D0437793

These
Unlucky
Stars

Also by Gillian McDunn

Caterpillar Summer
The Queen Bee and Me

McDunn, Gillian, author.
These unlucky stars

2021
33305252302926
sa   05/13/22

These Unlucky Stars

Gillian McDunn

BLOOMSBURY
CHILDREN'S BOOKS
NEW YORK LONDON OXFORD NEW DELHI SYDNEY

BLOOMSBURY CHILDREN'S BOOKS
Bloomsbury Publishing Inc., part of Bloomsbury Publishing Plc
1385 Broadway, New York, NY 10018

BLOOMSBURY, BLOOMSBURY CHILDREN'S BOOKS, and the Diana logo
are trademarks of Bloomsbury Publishing Plc

First published in the United States of America in March 2021
by Bloomsbury Children's Books

Text copyright © 2021 by Gillian McDunn
Illustrations by Jeanette Levy

All rights reserved. No part of this publication may be reproduced or transmitted in any form
or by any means, electronic or mechanical, including photocopying, recording, or any
information storage or retrieval system, without prior permission in writing from the publisher.

Bloomsbury books may be purchased for business or promotional use.
For information on bulk purchases please contact Macmillan Corporate and
Premium Sales Department at specialmarkets@macmillan.com

Library of Congress Cataloging-in-Publication Data
Names: McDunn, Gillian, author.
Title: These unlucky stars / by Gillian McDunn.
Description: New York : Bloomsbury Children's Books, 2021.
Summary: According to eleven-year-old Annie, luck is never on her side, causing her
to be somewhat of a loner, but after some prodding by her social studies teacher
Annie relunctantly tries her fortune at making friends.
Identifiers: LCCN 2020035095 (print) | LCCN 2020035096 (e-book)
ISBN 978-1-5476-0538-5 (hardcover) • ISBN 978-1-5476-0539-2 (e-book)
Subjects: CYAC: Self-confidence—Fiction. | Brothers and sisters—Fiction. | Luck—Fiction. |
Friendship—Fiction.
Classification: LCC PZ7.1.M43453 Th 2021 (print) | LCC PZ7.1.M43453 (e-book) |
DDC [Fic]—dc23
LC record available at https://lccn.loc.gov/2020035095

Book design by Jeanette Levy
Typeset by Westchester Publishing Services
Printed and bound in the U.S.A. by Berryville Graphics Inc., Berryville, Virginia
2 4 6 8 10 9 7 5 3 1

All papers used by Bloomsbury Publishing Plc are natural, recyclable products
made from wood grown in well-managed forests. The manufacturing processes
conform to the environmental regulations of the country of origin.

To find out more about our authors and books visit
www.bloomsbury.com and sign up for our newsletters.

For Leo

These Unlucky Stars

PART ONE

Oatmeal: Portrait of a Family in Four Bowls
From the Collected Drawings of Annie P. Logan

CHAPTER 1

You can measure how lucky someone is by asking them whether they believe in it.

Lucky people say, "There's no such thing."

To them, the universe is orderly and kind. Hard work always leads to happiness. Life goes according to plan. They never notice the million times their luck steps in to save the day.

My brother, Ray, is like this. He's a sunny-side-up, lemons-into-lemonade, golden-ticket kind of person. A real umbrella-remembering type.

I can hardly stand it.

The truth is, sometimes people try hard, but things don't go their way. Ma used to see that about me. I may mess up, but I'm always *trying*.

Unlucky Annie, she'd whisper, gathering the pieces of the green glass lamp.

Of course, she'd murmur, dabbing at my bloody knees with a cool washcloth.

Born under an unlucky star, she'd say, like it was a song we both knew by heart.

Then she went away, when Ray was five and I was only four. Kissed us both goodbye and coasted her pumpkin-colored station wagon out of our long and narrow driveway—gone in the blink of a turn signal. We haven't heard from her since.

Dad and Ray don't talk about Ma. They don't know I think about her all the time. I might be the only one who remembers the genius of spaghetti dinners eaten in the bathtub. I'm the only one who knows about those midnight thunderstorms where she and I huddled together on the plaid sofa, eating sliced plums. Who else would buy a preschooler squishy tubes of paint from the grown-up art store because *some things are worth it?*

She smelled like carrots fresh from the garden. Her hair was the exact color of a new penny.

I don't know if it's possible to wear out memories. She left before I had a chance to store up very many. My mind runs over the same ones again and again until they've almost gone smooth—like pebbles in the stream that winds behind our little house. At times I feel like I'm at the edge of remembering something more, something new—but it's always just out of reach, floating away like a balloon with a too-short string.

If she were here, I'd want to know everything—all the good things and bad things. I'd ask her if she ever felt unlucky, too. I already know she believes in luck. But I wonder if she thinks a person can be so unlucky, they act as a magnet for trouble—a lightning rod that draws every bad thing directly their way.

In other words: Am I the reason she left?

But I have no one to ask, so for now I keep that question in a quiet corner of my heart.

CHAPTER 2

It's probably true that given my track record for broken bones, broken *things*, and all-around bad luck in general, I have no business at all sitting on a roof.

But this roof is a good one.

It runs right outside my bedroom window and has the best view in all of Oak Branch, North Carolina. This is the spot where thick pine trees give way to a wide panorama of the Blue Ridge Mountains—also known as *my* mountains, because there's no one in the world who loves them like I do.

Each morning, the roof practically calls my name. "Annie, come take a look. Your mountains are shining real pretty today."

It's an extremely persuasive roof.

However, Dad is not easily swayed. "Come down," he'd argue. "You'll break your head."

But just like he needs coffee and oatmeal, I need my mountains and colored pencils to start the day. What Dad doesn't know won't hurt him.

I arrange my sketch pad on my knees and get to work making the lines of my mountains. Even though I have the peaks memorized, I'm never bored. Each time I see them, they show me something new. On hazy mornings like today, my mountains shimmer prettier than any old ocean. Evenings offer rainbow-swirl sunsets. And after bedtime, the sky turns to dark velvet with stars so bright, they look positively grabbable.

I lean against the wall, my back to Ray's bedroom window. Never in a million years would my brother join me out here. He's ten months older than I am and likes to point out that he's also ten months *wiser*. But the truth is that he has a real stubborn rule-following streak. He cares more about being the best at everything than he does about appreciating the simple fact that he's a hop, skip, and a jump from something downright glorious.

So this roof remains my own personal slice of heaven. Which is exactly how I like it.

"Annie! You'll be late!"

Dad's shout echoes up the stairs, bounces across my bedroom, and ricochets through my open window, finally landing square on me. I gulp, looking down at my drawing. I've been so deep in my thoughts that I've completely forgotten about that little thing called "school."

"In a minute!" I yell back. But instead of scrambling to pick up my pencils, I turn to my paper once more. Using my index finger, I smudge crisp lines to softness until the mountains on the page feel as full and alive as the ones in front of me.

Now I need to hurry. I gather my pencils and zip them into their pouch. The morning light catches the bumps and lines on the back of my hand—a constellation of scars, also known as the souvenirs from a dog bite when I was little. Even though they've mostly faded into things that can be felt more than seen, I always know they're there. And I still don't trust dogs. Not one bit.

"Annie!" Dad yells again in a "right now and I mean it" voice.

Yikes. He's louder now, his feet thudding on the staircase. I jump into action. Through the open window, I toss my pencil pouch and sketchbook onto my bed. The doorknob jiggles just as I aim one foot through the window. I freeze.

The door swings open, and Dad's shoulders fill the frame. His eyes widen as he takes in the scene. One innocent left foot planted on the scuffed wood floor. One guilty right foot out on the roof. That's me: half good intentions and half bad luck.

Dad pauses and I wait like that, wondering what will happen next. Today, like every morning, his dark hair is combed and his face is freshly shaved. Dad has no patience for the magic of crawling on roofs. He doesn't understand morning drawings or the way mountains call to me. In fact, he doesn't understand *me* at all. It's not his fault—he's practical. Predictable. If he were a food, he'd be oatmeal. If he were a color, he'd be beige.

The tips of his ears turn scarlet. My eyebrows pop up. I've never seen him lose his temper. It's not like I *want* him to yell at me—but if he did, I wouldn't mind it. At least then I'd know what he was feeling.

But the explosion doesn't come. Instead, he seems to swallow his fury. Instead of yelling, he lets out a sigh. "Annie, you know you can't be out there. Safety rules."

I try to think fast. "Dad, can we relax a few of those rules? I need this view like I need oxygen. It's not my fault that all these trees have grown up so big that I can't see my mountains from my window anymore—"

Dad shakes his head, cutting me off. "Not a chance. You'll break your head!"

Anger stirs in my chest. Just like always. Dad thinks I'm careless, a baby who needs to be protected—but he's wrong. I'm eleven years old, and I'm a lot more responsible than he gives me credit for. I may not be perfect but he doesn't see how hard I try.

I cross my arms. "I've been out on the roof every day this year and haven't come anywhere close to falling off. Not even once!"

When I realize what I've done, I clap my hands over my mouth. I can't believe I admitted to breaking his safety rules. My mind spins, trying to think of a way out.

"I mean—" I start.

A muscle in his jaw twitches.

"Later," he says. His eyebrows are still pushed together in a line. "Time for school. Your brother is waiting."

It's his "no use arguing" voice, which is *so unfair.* I bring my foot inside with a stomp and then shut the window with a *bang.*

I'm so mad that I barely notice the tinkling sound the glass makes. But no matter how mad I am, there's no mistaking what I did to my window. A crack splits sideways across it like a river searching for shore.

I wince. Late for school *and* a broken window? It looks like this is one of those days where my bad luck goes overboard.

In slow motion, Dad takes in a giant breath. It lasts so long, I think his lungs might pop. But then he lets it out in a whoosh.

"You can't get carried away like this," Dad says. "You're so careless sometimes."

Not careless. Unlucky. First that he caught me, then that the window broke.

I open my mouth, but he holds up his hand to stop me.

"I'll tape it up. Go on to school or you'll be late."

He rubs at his temples like he has a headache. I grab my backpack and head downstairs, taking the steps two at a time.

Ray waits by the front door. "You're late. *Again.* If you mess up my year, I will never forgive you."

I sigh. My brother is an excellent citizen. And by *excellent citizen*, I mean Excellent Citizen. Capitalized, like it is on the trophy he's won the last four years. Part of that award is perfect attendance with no tardies. Just my luck to end up with a brother who's the absolute opposite of me.

I scowl. "Not everyone is a human alarm clock."

But he's already stepped outside, leaving me talking to the door. I grab my sweatshirt and follow after him. He's practically halfway down the driveway already.

I shake my head. Walking to school is Dad's grand plan to establish our self-reliance and grit. I can't say that it's working. But I don't mind it on a day like today, when I get a little extra time to breathe in the pine-scented mountain air.

I catch up to him at the base of the driveway. "Hey." He doesn't answer.

"You can't be mad on such a gorgeous day. Don't you love the morning air?" I breathe in deep.

"Did you get in trouble for being on the roof again?" he asks.

I frown. "Not really. He was angry, but you know Dad. He never says much."

"Figures," he says flatly.

"You mean it *figures* I'd be unlucky enough to get caught," I tell him.

He shrugs. "More like stubborn as a rock. You know you aren't supposed to be out there."

I kick at a stone on the path. "I'm not stubborn. I'm *unlucky*."

Ray tilts his head at me. "Luck is just a way people explain bad choices."

That is such an annoying thing to say. My being on the roof with my mountains is *not* a bad choice. It's necessary. Essential. But I shouldn't be surprised that my brother doesn't understand me. He never has and never will.

"You wouldn't believe in a lucky star if one smacked you upside the head!" The words come out louder than I was expecting. I think Ray is going to get mad, but instead his forehead is lined in a thoughtful scrunch. He's quiet, almost like he's thinking it over. He's really listening to me this time.

"That's not true," he says slowly. I feel my hopes rise.

"Really?" I ask. My heart starts to beat faster. Finally, we're going to be able to talk about something important to me—something *real*.

Ray taps his chin. "If one of your stars smacked into me, I'd believe something all right."

I bite my lip. "You would?"

Ray grins. "I'd *believe* that I needed to get my head examined."

My hopes deflate like a three-day-old balloon. Ray and I will never see eye-to-eye.

He's got a million friends and I can barely get one to stick.

He can do any sport he tries, and I'm a walking disaster.

We even look different. Ray's hair is dark and wavy—like Dad's—while mine is light brown and straight like Ma's. He's tall and lean and I'm short and round. His skin is smooth and even, while mine is sprinkled with freckles like someone threw handfuls of confetti. And don't even get me started on the fact that he didn't need braces and has never had a pimple.

He and Dad are exactly the same. Which makes me think I must take after Ma.

If she had stayed, life would be easier. Right now, Dad, Ray, and I form a skinny, lopsided triangle. They're all the way over on one side, and I'm on the other. If Ma were here, she would help balance it out. I'm not saying our family was ever destined to form a perfect square. But at this point, I'd take a trapezoid.

We head to the narrow trail that shortcuts to school. The path threads between houses and requires hopping over a couple of low fences, but no one minds. The only drawback is that this time of year, there can be a whole lot of—

My foot slips, and I skid into a murky muddle the color of milk chocolate.

"Ugh!" I say, looking down at my new checkerboard Vans, which are soaking through quickly.

Ray's on the other side of the puddle. "Why didn't you jump over it like I did?"

I can't stand the pain of admitting I wasn't paying attention. I throw him a sour look and don't reply.

Gingerly, I move toward the edge of the lake of mud. *Please don't let me land on my rear end.* Finally, I make it to solid ground. The first thing I do is look at my shoes. They're probably stained forever, but later I'll throw them in the wash. For now, all I can do is try to wipe off the big blobs. I fish a tissue out of my pocket and lean over to work on my right toe—but as I do, I feel a minor avalanche cascading over my shoulders and head. The entire contents of my backpack—my folders, my library book, my homework for Ms. Palumbo, even my favorite pencil pouch—are now soaking in the mud.

Groaning, I clap my hands over my eyes. I can't bear to look.

"Well, don't just stand there!" Ray doesn't hide the irritation in his voice. I peek between my fingers and see him collecting everything piece by piece.

He holds up a dripping sheet of paper. "Your home-work is a goner."

The ink has run onto the pages and is unreadable. The library book jacket will wipe clean, but the pages are dotted with streaks and splashes of mud. The pencil pouch is disgusting, but I might be able to clean the pencils themselves. What a mess. I shove everything in my backpack.

"Make sure you zip it this time," Ray says.

"It *was* zipped—it came undone on its own!" Or maybe I was in such a hurry, I forgot. But I won't admit it, not even for a million dollars.

He rolls his eyes. "Yeah, sure. A zipped backpack magically opened when you leaned over. And that mud was out to get you, the way it jumped up and hit you in a tidal wave out of nowhere. It had *nothing* to do with the fact that you weren't watching where you were going."

He turns and starts walking away.

I hurry to catch up. "This is what I'm telling you! It's my bad luck. This kind of thing would never happen to you."

Ray kicks at the path, scattering tiny pebbles in front of us. "I'm not any luckier than you. The difference is that I don't blame the stars when bad things happen."

"How many library books have *you* ever dropped in the mud?" I ask.

He doesn't answer. Instead, he puts on a burst of speed and I'm hurrying again, my muddy shoes squishing with every step. I'm not perfect like Ray, and I never will be. My life would be easier if everyone understood that.

CHAPTER 3

He walks ahead of me. I don't bother hustling to catch up, because I know he'll have to wait to cross at Ledge Road—it's busy with cars, like it is every morning.

Most of the traffic heads in the direction of Mountain Ring. Almost none travels toward Oak Branch. Dad says that Mountain Ring is *booming*—it's being built up fast with expensive shops, fancy restaurants, and rows of houses on their mountainside. Two years ago, they opened their own schools and took all the Mountain Ring kids out of Oak Branch. Meanwhile, our little town struggles to keep its shops and schools going. It doesn't seem fair.

I was right—when I get to Ledge Road, Ray is standing there waiting for a gap in traffic. I come up next to him and am about to make a comment about how he shouldn't rush ahead just to spend time standing still. But before I can say anything, he reaches over and shoves a baggie into my hand.

It's a sandwich—Ray's usual turkey, lettuce, and mustard on whole wheat.

I peer at it doubtfully. My brother is a lot of things, but never have I known him to be a random sandwich giver.

I frown. "What's this for?"

He doesn't take his eyes off the street. "I thought you might like to eat today."

I go backward through my thoughts. Then, groaning, I smack myself on the forehead. He's right. After everything this morning with Dad and the window, I never packed a lunch. There's only one thing I can't figure out.

"How did you know?"

The corner of his mouth quirks up. "Your entire backpack just emptied out into a mud puddle, remember? I didn't see your bag."

I hesitate. "Are you sure? Won't you be hungry?"

Ray shrugs. "I have peanut butter crackers and raisins in my bag."

"Raisins! *Blech*," I tell him. Only Ray would pack *raisins*, of all things.

He doesn't say a word.

"Thanks," I say.

"Not a big deal," Ray says. "Come on—let's cross."

We step into the street, and something catches my eye—something on the road. At first I think it's a small rock. But then it *moves*. Sitting in the middle of the double-striped yellow lines is a tiny turtle.

I grab Ray's arm. "Look!"

Ray glances at it and shrugs. "Probably looking for water this time of year."

"Of all the roads to cross, this is the worst one possible," I say. "That's some bad luck right there."

Ray ignores me. We reach the path, and for a moment I'm swept along in the masses of kids heading to school. They're talking and swinging their backpacks. Ray starts to move more quickly, too—but I can't stop thinking about that turtle in the road.

I pull his sleeve. "Do you think it made it across?"

Ray frowns. "What are you talking about?"

I give him a look. "The *turtle*. It needs our help. We have to go back."

Ray lets out a big sigh, like he thinks I'm being ridiculous. "You don't even *like* animals. Quit trying to make me late."

"That's completely unfair," I say. "I do so like animals."

"Oh really," he says. "Since when?"

I cross my arms. "Since *now*."

He shakes his head. "What about dogs?"

I hold up my scarred hand. "Remember this? I have a good reason not to like dogs."

He squints at me. "Cats?"

"They make me itch," I admit.

"Birds?"

I shudder. "Creepy things descended from dinosaurs? No thanks."

"I've seen you flip out over bugs, so I'll assume that's a no," he says. "Same for lizards and bats."

"Other than that, though, I don't mind them one bit," I say.

He rolls his eyes. "For instance?"

I think fast. "Like deer. I see them in the woods sometimes, and they are real sweet with their babies. Or maybe, like, koalas? We saw that one at the zoo and it was really cute."

Ray turns to go.

"Or fish, Ray! I don't mind fish!" I yell at his back.

He doesn't even pause for a second. I know I should follow him, but the turtle is all I can think of. I'm on a mission.

As I head back to the busy road, my heart beats in my throat. I don't know what I'll do if she's been smashed by a car. I have decided the turtle is a she.

But when I get there, I breathe a sigh of relief. There she is, on the yellow lines like she's decided it's a grand place for a morning rest.

"That's a dangerous spot to linger," I tell her.

She blinks.

"Go on," I say. "Get yourself out of the road."

She doesn't budge.

I need to do *something.*

Before I can lose my nerve, I dash into the street. I reach down and scoop her right up. This startles her, and she tucks herself into her shell.

"It's okay," I tell her. "You're safe now."

But even as I'm saying the words, I feel a rumbling. I turn my head. Bearing down on us is an enormous truck, going way too fast. There's no time to move. I stand right there on the yellow stripes, squeeze the tiny turtle to my chest, and pray. It's not a prayer with words; it's more of a prayer with *feeling*—the feeling of: *please no, please no, please no, please no*—

The truck roars by with the blare of a horn.

"Get out of the road, kid!" a man yells out the window.

"Aw!" I yell back. "You get out of the road yourself!"

I glare at the retreating vehicle, already too far away to hear my reply

I check on the turtle, who I have decided to name Esmeralda. "We made it. Are you okay?"

Turtles don't nod, but she blinks again, and I think she's saying "Whew, that was a close one, but I'm fine." I hold her carefully, and in four jumps we are safe on the sidewalk. My heart is roaring and my breath is unsteady. But when I look at the turtle, she peeks out at me, smiling. Well, not *smiling* exactly. I don't know if turtles smile. But at least it's something like it.

I can't help grinning. "Well, aren't you cool as a cucumber after staring death straight in the eye."

She squints, which probably means "thank you" in her turtle language. It makes my heart fill up. We are understanding each other just fine.

I cradle her to my chest and walk farther on the trail to school.

Dad has a no-pets rule, but I wonder if I might keep her. She wouldn't take up much space. Maybe I could teach her some turtle tricks. She's already mastered squinting and blinking.

But Dad says *no exceptions*. Not even a hermit crab. Not even a goldfish. I could keep her on my roof. But that doesn't seem like it would be a good life for a turtle.

I reach the front of the school, which serves all the kids in Oak Branch up until high school, when we'll have to take the bus over to Mountain Ring. The courtyard is empty. I guess the final bell rang when I was saving Esmeralda. I head over to a patch of turf by the stream that meanders near the trail. Gently, I lower her to the grass.

"It's up to you," I whisper. "If you want to be wild, walk away. If you want to be with me, stay right where you are."

She pauses for a long moment. Maybe today is my lucky day. Maybe she'll be mine. But then she starts to stir. Before I know it—without even a blink—she crawls away.

As she disappears under a bush, my heart folds in on itself. *Goodbye, Esmeralda. You were almost a friend.*

I straighten, pulling my backpack onto my shoulder.

"Annie Logan," says a deep voice behind me.

When I turn around, Mr. Melendez is peering at me. He's the school principal, and right now his forehead is wrinkled like a walnut shell.

"Mr. Melendez," I squeak.

"Annie Logan," he says. "Why don't you follow me to my office?"

He says it like a question, but it's not the kind that wants an answer. It looks like my regular old bad luck just got a whole lot worse.

CHAPTER 4

I can't believe I'm late to school. I can't believe I got caught. The only thing I *can* believe? My terrible luck that got me here in the first place.

Mr. Melendez tells me he will be right back. He disappears down the hallway. Across from his desk are two orange plastic chairs. I lower myself into one. The seat is curved in a way that pinches my rear end on both sides. It is extremely uncomfortable.

I try to distract myself by looking at the art on Mr. Melendez's walls. "Distracting" is a good word for it. Instead of the usual inspirational posters or student work, Mr. Melendez has an assortment of unusual paintings. One is so bright, it almost hurts my eyes—a painting done entirely in shades of yellow and orange of two children with sinister expressions holding a bucket, standing on a hill. It seems like what might happen if someone crossed a nursery rhyme with a nightmare.

I shudder and keep looking around the room. Included on the walls are paintings of: a barn and a wheelbarrow of potatoes, a monkey-bear creature wearing a birthday hat, and, my personal favorite, a towering stack of pancakes next to a waterfall.

I am bursting with questions for Mr. Melendez—did he paint these? Did he *buy* them? Sure, some of them are terrible—but at least they're *interesting*. I'll give him credit for that. But when he returns, he's not alone. With him is Ms. Palumbo, my social studies teacher. The only thing I dislike more than social studies is Ms. Palumbo. If I could, I'd slide underneath this pinchy orange chair and hide.

Mr. Melendez sits behind his desk, and Ms. Palumbo pulls up the other orange chair. She's narrower than I am, so the sides don't squeeze her, but she perches on the edge of the seat anyway. She wears her black hair really short and today is wearing bold, geometric earrings in cadmium yellow.

"Thank you for waiting," says Mr. Melendez.

"It's not like I had a choice," I answer.

He raises his eyebrows sharply. Oops. I wasn't trying to have a smart mouth. Sometimes I can't draw the line between what I should say out loud and what I should keep to myself.

"Sir," I add, trying to recover.

He nods. I have noticed that sometimes a few well-placed *sir*s or *ma'am*s can go a long way—at least that's true here in Oak Branch.

Before answering, he straightens a stack of papers on his desk. "We wanted to take the opportunity to check in with you. Ms. Palumbo mentioned that your work is uneven."

My eyebrows draw together. So I'm not in trouble for being late—which should make me feel relieved. But it sounds like I'm in trouble for something else—maybe something worse.

I shift in my seat. "Not *all* my work. I have an A in art."

"Mmm," says Mr. Melendez. He says it like art doesn't count, which makes me fighting mad. He searches in his pile of papers. "Ah, yes, here it is. Your teachers report that you are withdrawn and have few friends. You sit alone at lunch. Does that describe you, Annie?"

My cheeks burn. I gulp, looking back and forth from Ms. Palumbo to Mr. Melendez. They're looking at me like a bug in a jar. How embarrassing.

Ms. Palumbo leans forward even farther, which makes her earrings swing so hard that they might fly off her ears. "I've seen this kind of thing before. Sometimes kids struggle when they have an exceptionally high-achieving older sibling."

Oh. This is about *Ray*—how he's good at everything and I'm not. How I will never be a citizen of excellence.

"We wondered if you might need a stronger support system for next year," she continues.

My insides are like an escalator, rising and falling at the same time. So I'm not here because I'm in trouble. I'm here because they think I *have* troubles.

"A couple of weeks ago, I called and chatted with your dad," Ms. Palumbo continues.

I raise my eyebrows. Dad never mentioned that.

Ms. Palumbo nods some more. I think her earrings might be hypnotizing me. "He said he wasn't concerned as long as your grades were okay. But in my experience, grades paint only part of the picture. You have wonderful thoughts, but your teachers want to see you participate more. And being socially isolated is yet another concern, especially with those teen years right around the corner."

"I-I'm not *isolated.*" I trip over the words. "I like to eat in the art room so I can draw."

Ms. Palumbo makes a *tsk* sound in her throat. "I saw how you struggled with the group project this semester. I know you blew up and walked out of class."

Every muscle in my body tenses up. Group projects are the absolute worst, and I don't know why anyone pretends differently. Any friendship that survives a group project should be considered a downright miracle.

"It's not *my* fault they couldn't appreciate my illustrated time line of ancient Greece," I tell her hotly. "Do you have any idea how many outer columns are in the Parthenon?"

They stare at me blankly.

"Forty-six," I say, answering my own question.

Ms. Palumbo arches her eyebrow at Mr. Melendez. This makes me even madder.

"Besides, I do have friends," I say. "I hang out with Ray and his friends all the time."

Ms. Palumbo whirls on me, eyes glowing in triumph. "Exactly! *Ray's* friends. Annie, you deserve to have your own friends. Have you ever tried taking the initiative and starting a conversation? Try saying 'hi' to someone!"

I look out the window, barely holding on to my last shred of patience. The buildings block the view of the mountains, which makes me feel doubly alone. What I really want to say is, "Wow, great advice, Ms. Palumbo. Talking to another human being and saying hello? I never would have thought of that one."

Ms. Palumbo starts patting my arm in concern. I squirm away from her as much as I can, but she doesn't get the hint. Each time she pats me, her earrings sway again. "I read in your file that Mom's not in the picture. Is that right?"

Inside, I get that floaty balloon feeling, like something is just out of reach. My eyebrows go into a line, one that says "back off." But she's waiting for me to answer—she wants me to confirm what she already knows.

"So?" I say from between clenched teeth.

Ms. Palumbo makes a clucking sound. "Sometimes growing up is tricky, especially without a mother figure."

My frown deepens. *A mother figure?* I open my mouth and close it again. For the moment, I seem to have forgotten what words are or how to use them.

Mr. Melendez pushes a pink piece of paper across the desk. "We have a program that could match you with a mentor. Someone to show you the ropes of, of—"

"Of becoming a woman!" Ms. Palumbo finishes triumphantly.

My stomach promptly coils into a ball. Ick, ick, *ick.* Why do adults always want to talk about puberty? It's so gross, and I can tell that any second now, someone is going to use the word "blossoming," as in "blossoming into a young lady." If that happens, I will definitely melt into the floor and die.

"I already have a mentor," I say quickly. "A great one! She's really good at . . ."

My thoughts spin wildly. "*Mentoring!* Yes. She's a good mentor who likes to . . . *mentor.* Almost every day, we mentor together."

They exchange a glance like they don't believe me. I better step it up.

I take a breath. "We both like art. And we talk about all kinds of things. It's really good for me. It's really good for my, ah, development."

Mr. Melendez riffles through the papers on his desk. "She's not named as your emergency contact. Is this a relative? A neighbor?"

"Yes," I say.

He looks at me blankly.

"Oh! She's, um, an aunt. And a neighbor. Like a neighbor-aunt. More of a family friend, you could say."

Ms. Palumbo narrows her eyes suspiciously. "What's her name?"

My neck starts to sweat. "Her name?"

Mr. Melendez holds his pencil, ready to write down my answer.

"Her name, good question. Her name is—" I look at the wall with the orange-and-yellow paintings. The two kids on the hill, like a terrifying version of Jack and Jill.

"Listen," says Ms. Palumbo smoothly. "In cases like these—"

"Jack—*Jackie*!" I say it loud enough that they both jump slightly in their chairs.

Mr. Melendez writes it down. "Jackie. And her last name?"

I glance at the farm painting on the wall with the wheelbarrow of potatoes. I gulp.

"Spuds?" It comes out in barely a whisper.

Mr. Melendez's brow wrinkles. "*Spuds?* How do you spell that?"

I can't believe I said *Spuds*. No one has the last name of Spuds. If they find out I made up Jackie, they'll definitely call Dad. I need to make it seem more real.

"I think with a Z?"

Mr. Melendez taps his pencil. "A Z?"

He says it like Zs can't be trusted.

I need to commit. Need to really sell it.

"Two Zs," I say firmly.

Mr. Melendez's forehead grows a few extra wrinkles.

Ms. Palumbo looks like she's ready to do a puberty intervention, right here in the principal's office.

There's no use in doing something halfway. If we surveyed turtles in the road, I'm positive that nine out of ten would agree.

I clear my throat. "I'll spell it for you. Z . . . P . . . U . . ."

I'm off to a good start. Mr. Melendez scribbles to keep up.

". . . D . . ."

Ms. Palumbo sniffs. My throat is suddenly dry.

". . . Z," I say.

Mr. Melendez blinks. He's holding his pencil like he thinks I'm not done.

"And then one more Z," I say, hoping that I sound more confident than I feel. "That's it."

He holds the paper in the air. "Z-P-U-D-Z-Z. Highly unusual."

Ms. Palumbo frowns. "So it's *three* Zs. Earlier you said two."

I gulp. "Yes, three Zs. But they aren't all together."

She taps the desk. "And how did you say it's pronounced?"

"Zpudzz," my voice squeaks. "It's Dutch-Romanian, on my mother's side."

"Ah," says Ms. Palumbo.

"Dutch-Romanian," says Mr. Melendez excitedly, like it suddenly makes sense. "Well, *of course.*"

"Of course," I answer. "Indeed."

Before they can answer, I launch myself out of the chair, slinging my backpack over my shoulder. "So, um. That's great. Thanks for checking on me and all. And you know, I better get to class. Thanks again. Have a great summer. Ma'am. Sir."

As I head for the door, I hold my breath. I'm sure they'll call me back, but they don't.

I close the door behind me. What a morning. First Esmeralda and now Jackie Zpudzz. The day has got to get better from here.

CHAPTER 5

The entire day passes in a blur. Even though school got out an hour ago, the words from Mr. Melendez and Ms. Palumbo spin through my mind like they're on a carousel.

I'm at Oak Branch Community Park, sitting at the picnic table by the basketball courts. I should be happy. The sun is warm against my back and my mountains are crisp against the sky. My book is wide open, and I've sketched the beginnings of a few of the players. I'm not always good at capturing the feeling of movement, but usually I'm happy to try.

Today feels different. Ms. Palumbo's words echo in my ears. These are Ray's friends—not mine.

Thwack. Thwack. Thwack.

Sure, they say "hey, Annie" when I show up. But the truth is, they never ask me to play. I'm a girl and I'm younger than they are. They let me tag along. They're friendly but not really my *friends.*

Ray's best friend, Grant, aims from the three-point line. When he lets go, it soars in a long arc before going through the hoop. His light skin is flushed red underneath his sweaty blond hair. Grant grins quietly, but red-headed Tyler races around the court like he was the one who made the basket. He waves his arms wildly. "Nothing but net! Nothing but net!"

Someone moves beside me—it's Faith, sitting on top of the picnic table. She used to be in Ray's grade at Oak Branch, but two years ago her family moved to Mountain Ring. For some reason, she's been hanging around the park every afternoon this week. Except for saying hi once or twice, we haven't talked. Friendly but not friends.

What did Ms. Palumbo say? *Take the initiative and start a conversation.*

She sits cross-legged. Her hair is in lots of skinny braids and she has medium-brown skin. She's wearing a green shirt.

Talking with Mr. Melendez and Ms. Palumbo was beyond weird, but maybe they had a little bit of a point about one thing. Maybe I do need a friend—one who's just for me.

She uncaps a bottle of turquoise fingernail polish. Each nail she paints the same way: first a stripe of color down the middle, then a little flick of the brush that pushes the polish to the edges. She stays inside the lines the whole time.

I'm tired of watching and waiting. I don't want to be stuck like a turtle in the road.

"Hey," I say before I lose my nerve.

Faith looks up. "Hey."

I clear my throat, not sure what to say next. "Is your family moving back to Oak Branch or something?"

She gets a look on her face that reminds me of shutters closing over a window. "No," she says flatly. "I'm staying with my aunt Louise for a while."

Okay, that did *not* go well. I should have known it wouldn't be as easy as saying hi. Thanks a lot, Ms. Palumbo.

We're quiet for a moment, watching the boys. Grant keeps looking over here and smiling. I don't think it's at me.

Faith blows on her fingers to dry them. Then she holds them in front of her. They sparkle in the sun.

"Tahitian Breeze," she says.

She talked to me! I can't mess this up.

I nod. "Well, it's a great color. Just . . . really . . . great. I like it."

Awkward. I'm about to go back to my sketchbook when she catches my eye. "Want me to do yours?"

I glance down at my nails, which are raggedy and have a little dirt under them. I wish I could blame that on this morning's mud puddle, but I can't. They usually look like this.

"Okay," I say, wiping my hands on my pants.

She motions for me to sit on the picnic table, too, so I climb up next to her. She grabs my hand and peers at it carefully. Working steadily, she moves from one finger to the next, occasionally tilting my hand to a better angle. It's a strange feeling but not a bad one. When she finishes with one hand, I reach out with the other.

She stares at my skin, tilting her head sideways. "What happened here?"

My scars. I pull my hand away fast—too fast. I jostle her arm, causing the bottle of Tahitian Breeze to fly through the air, finally landing upside down on the ground with a sickening *crack*. My cheeks get hot. Another bit of bad luck. Just when I was making a friend. Just when I was feeling normal.

Faith hops off the table and grabs the bottle. It's not broken, but a lot of the polish spilled out.

"I'm so sorry," I say.

Faith twists the cap back on. "I didn't expect you to jump away, that's all."

My face burns. "I'll buy you a new one."

She shrugs. "There are worse things in the world."

Faith sits on the table again and reaches for my hand. When she sees the surprise on my face, she smiles.

"I'm pretty sure I have enough. Okay?"

I nod. This time she doesn't ask about my scars. She paints my nails with quick, confident strokes.

Usually, I don't talk about what happened with my hand. Maybe it's my contrary nature, but the fact that she isn't asking sure makes me feel like telling.

I clear my throat. "My hand is scarred because a dog bit me. In this park, actually."

Faith's eyes widen and she looks around, like the dog could show up any minute. *"Where?"*

I point with my chin at a cluster of maple trees on a grassy ridge. "Ma used to bring Ray and me here all the time and lay out a blanket. She stepped away for a minute, and a dog came over and chomped my hand. Walked right past my brother, of course, and picked me to bite. That's the kind of luck I have."

Ma used to take us here to look at the view. We'd have picnics with a big jar of lemonade and freezer waffles. Ray and I used to roll down that hill until we were dizzy. Afterward, we'd visit the band shell, which used to have concerts all summer long. These days it's a little run-down and could use a coat or two of paint, but back then it was the most fabulous place my little-kid self could imagine.

Faith's still staring at my hand, her forehead crinkled in worry. "It must have hurt a lot."

"Sometimes they itch or feel tight. But when I was little, I used to wish— Never mind." I stop myself from finishing the sentence because I'm afraid it sounds silly.

Faith looks at me sideways. "Did you wish it was a *magic* scar? Like one that could tell the future?"

I wince, nodding. It sounds babyish, hearing it out loud like that.

Faith frowns. "My mom says it would be a burden to know the future—that we wouldn't like it if we had that power."

She says the words casually, like she knows millions of things about her mom. She probably *does*—she probably even knows what her mom ate for breakfast today. The thought of it makes my head fill up with questions like floating balloons. I don't know what Ma thinks about the future. I only know she wanted one without me in it.

"But for me, I'd want to know. Would you?" Faith's voice is serious, almost solemn.

"I'd want to know," I say. "I don't like not knowing things."

Faith nods once, like we decided something important. "Me too."

It feels like a puzzle clicking into place. She shows me how to blow on my fingernails to dry them, and I do. We watch the boys play. Ray makes an easy shot and Tyler scowls. They're on different teams.

Faith bumps my shoulder. "Which one do you like?"

I wrinkle my nose. "None of them."

She rolls her eyes. "But what if you had to pick one?"

"I guess . . . Javier?" He's the nicest of Ray's friends. Plus, I like his freckles and superlong eyelashes even if I don't *like* him.

Faith nods. "Those eyes, right?"

I smile and she grins back. Maybe this is easier than I thought.

"What about you?"

She sighs and shakes her head. "When I lived here before, I liked Jordan—but not anymore."

"Grant was looking over at you earlier," I say.

Faith's eyes get big. "Really? Hmmm."

When the sun gets low in the sky, it's time for Ray and me to go meet Dad for dinner. I say bye to Faith, and she says "see you later" with a wave of her turquoise-painted fingernails that match mine exactly.

We're not real friends—not yet. But at least it's something like it.

CHAPTER
6

The quickest way to Oak Branch's downtown is to take the wooden pedestrian bridge that runs right over Glass Lake, which is surrounded on three sides by mountains. There's a chill in the air, so I pull on my favorite green sweatshirt. By the time we make our way across, the sun is low in the orange-sherbet sky. Beyond the lake, my mountains oversee it all—the purpling clouds, the deep blue water, my brother, and me.

Our town is small, and it's seen better days. Some shop windows are boarded and vacant, and there aren't as many people walking around as there used to be. But I love it anyway—it has everything we need. We get our groceries at Quinn's Market, which closes early on Fridays. They've already brought their baskets of produce and flowers indoors. Oak Branch Books is a yellow building with big windows that look out on the water. The shelves run all the way to the ceiling, and there's a tree house inside that you can climb up into.

Dad's hardware store sits on the corner. It's called Logan & Son, which is what it's been called since Grandpa Floyd built it forty years ago. Dad was a baby then, but Grandpa already knew that his son would take over the business someday. And I guess someday Ray will run the store, too.

Once, I asked him why he didn't change it to Logan & Son & Daughter, and he just sighed. "Annie, this is how it's been and how it always will be."

Practical. Predictable. The answer of a man who eats oatmeal for breakfast every day.

There are three restaurants in town. One is called H. Diggity. It's painted blue and has pennants hanging in the windows. They serve hot dogs with homemade relish, salty french fries, and fresh-squeezed lemonade. Lulu's is a coffee shop in a white brick building with crisp black awnings. They make my favorite corn muffins and serve them with strawberry butter.

The third restaurant is called JoJo & The Earl's and it's my favorite. They serve Carolina barbecue seven days a week. There's no place like it in the world. And that's where we are meeting Dad for dinner, like we do every Friday.

JoJo & The Earl's is a long, narrow building that is painted red and yellow. The awnings are striped red and yellow. Even the flowers in the planter boxes are red and yellow! Inside is more of the same: half the restaurant is red and half of it is yellow. On one side, all the tables, seats, curtains, and walls are red. And on the other, yellow.

When we step inside, Ray and I help ourselves to the root beer barrel candy that's kept in a glass dish at the register and is free to anyone who wants a piece. The Earl is busy taking orders from a table of people we don't recognize, probably out-of-towners. I love The Earl, who looks like Santa, except minus the white beard and plus a big old Southern accent.

JoJo comes out from the back, carrying a couple of her famous chess pies. Her silver hair is in an updo held with pretty red and yellow clips. When she sees us, she beams.

"Let me get these in the case, and then I'm going to hug you both up," she says. JoJo's hugs are round and soft, just like JoJo.

She peers at us both. "I do believe you two have grown since last Friday."

"Now, darlin'," The Earl says from across the restaurant. "Don't fuss too much at those young folk, or you'll scare them off."

"Hush, you," she says back, but she's not cross. Her voice is sweeter than all the pies in the case. She twinkles her special smile at The Earl, and he grins right back.

The restaurant is small enough that we can hear The Earl explaining. "You can order from either side of the menu, no matter where you sit. Yes, it's unusual to serve both Eastern and Western barbecue at the same restaurant. But people do unusual things when love is concerned." He catches JoJo's eye and gives her an exaggerated wink. She shakes her head and rolls her eyes a bit, but she's smiling.

The Earl turns back to his table. "North Carolina barbecue is a serious business, some would even say contentious. The eastern part of the state likes vinegar barbecue sauce, and the western part of the state likes Lexington style, which is made with an *absolutely delicious* red sauce, from a recipe that's been handed down from one generation to the next."

"Now, don't let him talk you out of the vinegar," JoJo calls. "You should at least give it a try."

When my dad was little, The Earl was a young man and the restaurant was called simply "The Earl's." Famous for Western-style barbecue and red slaw made from The Earl's great-granny's secret formula. The restaurant was long but narrow, as it is today—only two tables wide. But back then, everything was painted red—exactly like the sauce they were famous for.

But years later, after my dad was grown and The Earl was even older, something amazing happened. The Earl fell in love with JoJo McCoy, our JoJo. The only trouble was that JoJo was from the eastern part of the state, far from the mountains and way down near the water where they do everything different, including their barbecue. JoJo liked *vinegar* barbecue only and couldn't abide red sauce. She said she couldn't work in a Western-style barbecue restaurant, even though she was admittedly in love with The Earl.

The Earl had to find a way to solve the problem. He closed the restaurant for four whole months. He moved east and learned from the best pitmasters in the region. He learned to make the vinegar and pepper sauce, without the slightest smidge of tomatoes. When he was ready to propose to JoJo, he asked her family for their support. And before they gave it, he had to make a meal that was up to standards.

It goes without saying that he earned their blessing. When JoJo and The Earl moved back to Oak Branch, they decided they would serve both kinds of barbecue. Which meant the restaurant needed some changes. JoJo sewed gingham curtains for every window, and they painted half the restaurant yellow.

The other big change was JoJo adding pancakes to the menu. She said she couldn't bear to be part of a restaurant that didn't serve pancakes.

Ray and I plop down at our favorite table—a four-seater in the exact middle where the red half and the yellow half meet each other. The table is painted half and half, too. I sit on the yellow side, and Ray sits on red. Swinging my legs, I let the spicy-sweet root beer candy melt on my tongue as I look at the menu. After all, looking at the menu is a Friday night tradition—even though we both have it memorized.

JoJo brings over our drinks—lemonade for me, an unsweet tea for Dad, and an Arnold Palmer for Ray, which is a fancy way of saying half lemonade and half tea.

"Your dad coming along in a bit?" she asks.

Ray and I nod. Dad running late to dinner is nothing new. He would never rush a customer out of the store, even if it means working after closing time.

She places a fistful of root beer candy between us. "Don't forget to save a little room for dessert," she says.

Ray and I grin at each other. No matter how full we are, we can always make room for a slice or two of JoJo's pie.

I'm on my second lemonade and my eighth root beer candy by the time Dad joins us.

The Earl ambles over to take our orders. He pushes his thick black glasses up on his nose and winks. "How's my favorite Friday night family?"

Even though he says it to everyone, I think he means it extra for us.

After we finish ordering, The Earl tucks his pen behind his ear and looks at Dad. "You told them the news?"

Dad smiles. "Not yet."

After The Earl walks away, Ray and I look at Dad. He sips his tea with an innocent look on his face.

"*What* news?" I ask. Ray's too polite to be so direct, but politeness doesn't get questions answered.

Dad puts down his glass. "You know Oak Branch is losing all its tourist trade to Mountain Ring. The town council is working on creating our own draw here in Oak Branch."

I scrunch my forehead. "Mountain Ring is so *fancy*. How can Oak Branch compare?"

Ray frowns at me. "That sounds disloyal, Annie."

He makes it sound like I should be tried for treason.

I glare back at him. "Don't blame me. I love Oak Branch more than anyone. It's not my fault that Mountain Ring is more popular."

"We have a wonderful downtown, hiking trails to the Big Little Waterfall, and the best view of the Blue Ridge Mountains," Dad says, sounding just like a brochure at our dilapidated visitors' center. "But we're small. As a town, we've been struggling. We're hoping this festival will put Oak Branch on the map."

"What festival?" Ray and I ask at the same time.

Dad's eyes shine. "The Rosy Maple Moth Festival."

He says it like he thinks we'll burst into applause. But instead, Ray and I look at each other. Dad's lost his mind.

"Sparksville has a Firefly Festival," Dad continues. "And Elwindale has Ladybug Fest. We thought this could do the same thing for Oak Branch."

Ray looks sideways at me. I grimace back.

"With *moths*?" I ask.

Dad frowns. "What's wrong with moths?"

"Dad," I say patiently. "People *like* fireflies and ladybugs. I've never met anyone who likes moths. Right, Ray?"

Dad looks perplexed. "Son, back me up. Moths are as important as any other creature."

Ray grimaces. "Yeah, but a whole festival? I don't know, Dad . . . they're kind of ugly."

Finding myself and Ray on the same side of an issue is so unusual, I'm stunned into silence.

"The rosy maple isn't *any* moth," Dad says. "You know which ones I'm talking about, right?"

Ray shakes his head. "Never heard of them."

"Me neither," I say.

Dad pulls his phone from his pocket. When the page loads, he holds it out to us. "Behold, the rosy maple!"

I'm afraid of what I'll see but still lean forward for a closer look. Ray does the same. When we see it, we gasp.

The rosy maple moth is *beautiful*.

I know I'm not much of a bug person, but I thought I knew moths. Every moth I've ever seen was a muted grayish brown—the exact color of dust. But the rosy maple moth is something else entirely. I can't stop staring at it.

The rosy maple moth is *not* the color of dust. It's hot pink and bright yellow. It looks like it was crayoned with the brightest colors in the box. My fingers itch to draw it—I'm already planning how to match the bright hues of this funny, furry little creature.

"These moths are from around here?" I ask, disbelieving.

Dad nods. "Sometimes they're overlooked, just like Oak Branch."

"They look like dessert," I say.

I expect Ray to laugh, but instead he agrees. "Like a lemon-strawberry ice-cream bar."

Dad tucks away his phone. "The festival will be held downtown, by the lake. With a big parade that ends in the band shell for a night of dancing, food, and fun. Each store is going to sponsor a float."

A float! This sounds like something I could help with. Dad and Ray are good at building, but they don't have any sense for what things should look like. I start thinking of what shades of paint will match the vibrant moth.

The Earl brings our food. He slides my plate of Eastern-style barbecue with boiled potato and corn sticks in front of me. Meanwhile, Ray and Dad dive in to their Western-style trays with slaw and extra hush puppies.

"I heard y'all talking about the festival," he says excitedly. "It's going to be something else!"

Dad and Ray nod, mouths already full.

"Ray's going to be my helper with fixing up the band shell," Dad says. "And with constructing the float."

I look up from my food. "Wait. If Ray's going to help build the float, what am I going to do?" I can hear the edge in my voice, but this is important. He better not say that I'll be the one working in the store while Ray is doing all the fun stuff.

Dad frowns, chewing thoughtfully. "I didn't think you'd be interested."

"Just because my name's not on the sign doesn't mean I don't care," I say. "I want to help design and paint it. Okay, Dad?"

He pauses, and I wonder for a moment what would happen if Ma were here. I have a feeling she would understand how important art is to me. It's more than important—it's essential.

Dad wipes his mouth with a napkin. Then he starts to nod. "You know, that may not be a bad idea. You can put all that art stuff to good use."

I'm so excited, I ignore his comment about *that art stuff*. My insides are flipping like flapjacks. If I design a float for the store, he'll have to notice how important art is to me.

I ask to see Dad's phone so I can look at the image search again. My favorite picture is one with a moth looking right at the camera, lifting one of his front legs like he's waving to say, "Here I am!"

Here I am, little moth. I can't wait to design a float that shows the world how cute you are.

This is going to be the best summer ever.

CHAPTER
7

The last week of school passes like every other last week of school in the history of time: s l o w l y.

I avoid Ms. Palumbo and Mr. Melendez the best I can. The school clocks slow to a crawl—sometimes I swear the minute hand actually moves backward. But eventually it's the last day of school. When the final bell rings, I'm officially a seventh grader.

I head to the park with Ray, like always. The day is steamy. Even the pine trees look droopy.

As I get closer to the basketball court, my heart droops, too. Three other girls sit on the table with Faith: Nailah, Emily, and Alicia.

Nailah and Emily are in Ray's grade and I don't know them well. But Alicia is one of the girls who was in that group project in Ms. Palumbo's class. Her hair is always perfect and the crusts on her sandwiches are always cut off. Just seeing her puts me in a bad mood.

The four of them take up all the room at the table. Finally, Emily scoots over so I can squeeze in at the end. Faith nods hi, but Nailah is in the middle of a long story.

I don't belong here. Maybe I should take out my sketchbook, but I don't want to answer any questions about it. These girls all know how to put on eye shadow and have favorite celebrities and take endless selfies. There's no way I can keep up when I don't even have a phone.

I find a piece of lint on my T-shirt to pick at. I keep hoping Faith will offer to do my nails again, but she doesn't.

After a while, Ray jogs over. "Let's take off. It's too hot for basketball. Besides, we have to help with festival stuff."

Alicia cuts her eyes at Ray. "I thought you were Annie's brother, but you sound like her dad." Nailah and Emily laugh.

Ray flushes. He picks up his backpack from the picnic table. When he does, I see that he left a paper underneath it, laid carefully so it wouldn't wrinkle or blow away. Then I realize that it's his Excellent Citizen award. Somehow I forgot that he would receive it today.

My insides prickle and flash. *I* want an award with my name on it in a curving script. It feels like a fire flaring, like something cracking and sparking from somewhere deep inside. It's not Ray's *fault* for winning, not exactly. But why does everything come so easily for him?

I scowl, folding my arms tight. "Don't tell me what to do."

Ray rolls his eyes. "You're being ridiculous."

I don't like him talking to me that way, especially around Faith. I don't want her to think of me as a baby. "You aren't my dad."

Ray glances at Alicia, who smirks. He opens his mouth like he's going to say something. But then he shrugs like it's no big deal. "Suit yourself."

I try not to watch him as he heads to the lake bridge, toward downtown. When he goes, a few of the others drift off. Some of the seventh graders say they're going to Quinn's Market for ice cream.

Nailah and Emily tell Alicia about something that happened in homeroom. I pick at the chipped paint on my nails and listen for a place where I might join in. I feel stuck in the middle, not sure how to move forward. A turtle in the road.

There are only three boys left on the court, tossing the ball aimlessly. Grant, Ray's friend who likes Faith. Javier with the famous dimples. And then there's Tyler, the loud, redheaded one.

As I watch, they turn and head toward us. They move in slow motion, almost like it's a coincidence that they happen to be heading this way.

I wonder if Faith is nervous, since she maybe likes Grant. But when they come over, she acts really casual.

"What's up?" she says.

I wish I could be like that.

Grant grins and his eyes crinkle up. Even though there're so many of us standing around, it also somehow feels like a private conversation between Grant and Faith.

"Too hot today," he announces.

"Let's do something else," Tyler says. He's standing right by me and smells like sweat.

"Like what?" Nailah asks.

"Truth or Dare?"

"Yes!" Emily ends the word almost in a hiss.

"Nah," Grant says.

"Never Have I Ever?" Tyler asks.

"Tyler. Relax," Grant says.

Tyler shifts from one foot to the other, like he can't stand still. "How about Ding-Dong Ditch?"

No one answers. He reaches out and pokes me in the arm. "What do you think? Ding-Dong Ditch?"

"I don't know what that is," I say. I look over at Grant and Faith, but they're smiling at each other, in their own world.

Tyler steps away from me and looks at the sky. "I can't believe it. I can't believe this girl doesn't know Ding-Dong Ditch."

Alicia shakes her head. "Tyler, don't make such a big deal about it." She turns and looks at me. "Ding-Dong

Ditch is when you ring someone's doorbell and then run away before they answer."

Tyler pokes me in the arm again. "You should do it. Go on, do it right now!"

"Don't bother her, Tyler," Nailah says. "She's a sixth grader."

I don't think Nailah means it in a rude way, but the last thing I want to feel right now is little, especially in front of Faith. I notice that Nailah has on turquoise nail polish, too. I wonder if Faith painted her nails and feel a little stab of jealousy.

"Seventh grader," I say evenly. "Same as Alicia."

Nailah rolls her eyes. "Oh, okay. *Seventh* grader. As of forty-five minutes ago."

This makes me feel even younger. I hate it.

I stand up quickly, before Tyler can poke my arm another time. "I'll do it. Where?"

Tyler hoots, rubbing his hands together. He points to a row of houses across from the park. "One of those! Ring the bell, then run away fast into the woods so no one catches you."

As I cross the street, little jolts of worry run up and down my legs. My feet are unsure. But I know I need to keep going.

Two of the houses are in clear view of the playground. But there's a third house where the front door is blocked by trees. I glance back at the playground and see that I have an audience. It would be my luck to fall over a crack in the sidewalk, right in front of everyone. I turn toward the house that's hidden from view and head up its driveway.

It's a little yellow house, much smaller than the tall trees surrounding it. The grass is scrubby with weeds and has wide patches of plain dirt. The screen door has been covered with layers of paint over the years. The finish is cracked and peeling enough that I catch glimpses of the previous layers peeking through: black, red, sky blue, and even an unfortunate yellow the exact color of dried-out mustard. It all clashes terribly with the graying walls of the house. I glance around. Terra-cotta pots hold crispy plants that are about four months past dead. The empty driveway is cracked, and the mailbox hangs at a precarious angle. No signs of life—maybe the house is vacant. The thought makes me feel braver. I'll just ring the bell and hurry back to the park.

I step onto the little porch and reach toward the doorbell. Then I hear a low growl.

I look down. Before, I'd been so busy looking at the peeling paint on the screen door that I hadn't realized that the door behind it was open a few inches. And now, from inside the house, a big dog is staring at me. There's only a thin mesh screen between us.

I freeze, my arm outstretched. The dog could easily push through the screen if he wanted to. He squints at me, ears flat against his head. His mouth is open wide enough to show me his monster teeth, which overlap and stick out at crooked angles. He's big and hairy and has eyes like laser beams.

I swear my hand tingles as I look at those teeth. A wild thought enters my head—maybe I have a magic scar after all. But I don't need fortune-telling abilities to know what would happen if this dog caught hold of me: he would rip me to pieces. I shudder.

The dog narrows his eyes. And then he starts to bark.

At least, I think it's a bark. I'm no expert on dogs, but I've never heard anything like this. It has a curve to it, starting out low and hoarse but ending in a yelp. And it's not quiet. The volume is turned all the way up—and somehow, the sound makes my teeth vibrate like the dog is a living, breathing dental drill.

I have to get out of here. But my feet feel glued to the floorboards.

He nudges the screen door, which strains against his weight. With each bark, little flecks of foam fly from his mouth and stick to the screen. I'm hypnotized by his teeth. I know what I need to do: back slowly away from this little crooked house and never ever come back again. But no matter how many times my brain crackles that message, it's like my wires are loose. My feet refuse to behave.

He pushes against the screen again, and finally I move backward, pulling my hand to my side.

Then I hear a woman call, "Otto, hush!"

Otto? This dog seems more like he'd be named Killer or Crusher. His barks echo in my ears. I need to get out of here.

"*Otto!* What is all that fuss?" The sound is louder now, closer to the door. Her voice is high-pitched and wobbly. She's old, I realize, and probably frail. There's no way she is strong enough to handle a beast like Otto.

The dog scrabbles his paws on the screen, like he'd like to jump through and see what a big chomp of Annie Logan would taste like.

But then, from inside—a *crash* and a *thud*. A solid sound, like something hitting the floor.

Otto doesn't notice or care. He continues to bark like he'd like to eat my face.

Then the wobbly voice calls out again. "Help! Help me! Is anyone there?"

A prickling feeling spreads from my stomach to my throat. I stand completely still.

I don't know what to do. But I know I need to do *something*.

PART TWO

The Lonely House
From the Collected Drawings of Annie P. Logan
Dimensions: 4" × 6"

CHAPTER
8

My thoughts spin. The dog turns and disappears into the house. I step sideways to the window. An old woman is sprawled across the floor, facedown. *Oh no.* It's my fault. I should never have listened to those kids at the park. She fell because of me—bad-luck, magnet-for-trouble me. What have I done?

The dog circles her, whining. What if she's unconscious? I should run back to the park, borrow a cell phone, and call 911—but before I can take a step back from the window, the old lady looks up at me. Her eyes are fiercely blue.

"Hey!" she hollers. "Hey!"

Otto starts barking, and I jump back from the window. "I'm going to call for help! Be right back."

Otto, barking and crying, runs from the lady to me at the window, then back again. He seems to be deciding what he'd like to do first—comfort his owner or have me for lunch.

The woman is moving. Maybe I won't need to call for an ambulance after all. Slowly, she props herself on her left arm, wincing. I have a better look at her face now. Her hair billows upward in a white tuft that reminds me of cotton balls, but her eyes are sharp. She's not some delicate old lady who needs rescuing. She's spitting mad. At *me*.

"Don't you go anywhere! You can't leave me like this!"

The dog nudges her, licking her other arm.

"Are you okay?" I ask. After the words are out, I wince. It's clear she's pretty far from okay.

Her eyes narrow. "Do I *look* okay?" She indicates her right arm. "I think it's broken."

My heart, which was beating a million beats a minute, suddenly turns to thick, sticky sludge. "Are you sure? Maybe it's only bruised."

But even as I say the words, I know they're wrong. Her right arm bends at a funny angle, and I haven't seen her move her fingers once.

She squints at me. "I didn't realize they handed out medical degrees to fourth graders."

My cheeks burn. I hate it when people assume I'm younger because I happen to be short. "I'm in *seventh* grade." As of this afternoon anyway. Is it possible that school let out only an hour ago? It feels like I've been standing on this porch for at least a year.

She sighs. "Fine, then. Old enough to help me find my hand phone. Where is my hand phone? Have you seen it?"

I pause. What in the world is a *hand phone*?

"I'm sorry—have I seen what?"

Her eyebrows pull together in a frown. "My hand phone!"

The room is cluttered and jumbled, with boxes on the floor and trinkets covering every surface. I have no idea what I'm looking for. An old-fashioned phone? Or maybe a watch? It could be anything.

"There it is!" she says. With a knobby finger, she points to a black rectangle on the floor, about five feet away. A regular old cell phone. It must have skittered across the floor when she took a spill.

"That's not a hand phone," I say. "It's a *cell* phone."

She scowls. "That's what I said! I need you to get it for me."

Maybe she bumped her head. Maybe I need to call a doctor. I open the latch on the screen door. But the moment I do, Otto lets out a low growl. I step backward.

I gulp. "The thing is, your dog hates me. So I'm going to go find a phone. Give me the number and I'll call for you."

"*Pish*," she says in a no-arguing-allowed voice. "I don't have Albert's number memorized. It's in the thingy."

Of course. His number is in the phone, so she needs that one. I have to help her. Even as my brain searches for another answer, I know I'm stuck.

I reach out for the door again. This time, Otto doesn't growl. Instead, he starts barking loud enough that they can probably hear him all the way in Mountain Ring.

"Hush, Otto. Now, what's got into you?" she says softly. She reaches out with her good arm and loops her fingers through his collar. She winces as she does it. Her arm must hurt something awful. The effort makes a sheen of sweat pop out on her forehead, but she manages to bring him close.

She murmurs something to him. I can't make out the words, but whatever she says seems to calm him. He sighs and sits down. This time, when I reach for the screen door, he doesn't make a sound.

Before my bravery slips away, I open the door and step inside.

Otto looks at me out of the corner of his eye. He's not happy that I'm there, but at least when he's quiet, his mouth is shut. I shudder, taking in a deep breath.

Every house has a smell. This one has no hint of the mountain air outside—it's like baby powder mixed with chicken soup and breath mints. Underneath it all is a smell I don't have a word for except "old." It's a packed-up-and-put-away kind of smell.

Cardboard boxes are stacked two and three high all around the room. There are a few paths between the boxes—an aisle from the front door to the kitchen, an offshoot to a flowered recliner chair that faces a television—but most of the floor is covered. I can barely walk without tripping—no wonder she fell.

"Are you moving out or something?" I ask.

She makes a huffing sound, like she's offended. "Just help me get up."

I hold out my hand, not sure what to do, and she grabs it. Her grip is surprisingly strong.

She looks me over from top to bottom. "Round little thing, aren't you?"

A bunch of not-nice words crowd in my head. I don't like it when people comment on my body. But now does not seem like the right time to tell her that, so I bite back my words.

She frowns. "What's your name anyway?"

"Annie P. Logan," I say, suddenly nervous. I don't know why I give her my middle initial like that.

She peers at me.

"Ma'am," I add for good measure.

She sniffs. "Gloria Crumb. So *very* pleased to make your acquaintance."

Her words are polite, but her tone is triple-coated in sarcasm. There's something about her that makes me want to comb my hair and tuck in my shirt. And I *never* tuck in my shirt.

I try to help her up, but it isn't easy. She twists herself sideways, moaning and grimacing more with every inch. I jostle her arm once, and she lets out a yell. The whole time, the dog makes little snuffling sounds but doesn't bark once. It's almost as if he can tell I'm trying to help her. I keep my eyes on her and not on his teeth.

Eventually, I help her into a sitting position. She wants me to help her stand, but I worry that I'll drop her.

She blows out an exasperated breath but seems to settle for sitting on the floor, leaning against the wall. "At least Albert won't find me on my back like a bug that can't flip over. He already thinks I'm too old to be living alone."

"Do you want a pillow, Mrs. Crumb?" I ask.

"Call me Gloria or nothing at all," she says sharply. "I won't abide by any of that *Mrs. Crumb* or *ma'am* nonsense. Those words are the domain of mealymouthed sycophants."

My eyebrows go up. "I may be a lot of things, but I'm not a psychopath."

She sighs. "What *do* they teach children at school these days? A sycophant is someone who flatters to gain favor. A toady. A kiss-up—do you know that one?"

I bristle. "I am not a kiss-up, either."

She nods crisply, then grimaces in pain. "So you know that one, at least. You aren't a total lost cause."

I frown. "Hey!"

She looks around. "Now, where is that hand phone?"

I pick it up and give it to her.

"Cell phone," I say. I admit it, my tone is smug. But I can't help it.

She glares at me. "That's what I *said*."

It's not worth arguing. She swipes and presses until she manages to find his contact information. When the number dials, a picture appears of a black-haired man holding a chubby baby.

I keep an eye on the dog. He's extremely odd. Odd Otto. I'd call him ugly, but that would be too easy. His hairiness level is extreme—it grows in tangles all over his body. His eyes point in different directions. His jaw is oversized, and his spiky teeth stick up over his top lip. And even though his mouth is closed, his tongue sticks out the side. There must be a gap in his teeth. *His teeth.* I shudder, taking a half step away from Otto and his mouth.

I can hear the phone ringing. *Come on, Albert. Pick up.*

Gloria Crumb pulls her head away. She frowns, like something occurred to her. "Annie *Logan*. Your dad owns the hardware store?"

I nod.

"That HomeMade in Mountain Ring has better prices," she says.

Now, this I can't let go. At my house, HomeMade is like a bad word. As the number of customers at Logan & Son gets smaller and smaller, the worry creases in Dad's forehead get deeper and deeper.

I fix her with a look. "Lots of people would rather buy twelve cheap light bulbs at HomeMade than one regular-price one at a local family business."

Then I smile sweetly, which seems to throw her off. She returns to her call for a moment, then presses the button to disconnect. Her frown adds extra wrinkles to her face.

"Well, Annie P. Logan, we have ourselves a problem. Albert isn't answering."

I chew my lip, thinking. "We could call the emergency number."

She sniffs. "Not on your life. I don't need everyone in town knowing my business."

"We could wait and try Albert later." But when I catch sight of her bad arm, it's turning colors faster than a summer sunset. That can't be good.

"Pish," she says. "I think I need a doctor." I can tell she hates admitting it.

We need someone to help. Someone steady. Someone reliable. Someone who always knows what to do.

I pick up the phone and make my fingers dial.

CHAPTER
9

Faster than a hot knife through butter, Dad shows up on Ms. Gloria Crumb's front porch. Ray's not with him, so I'm guessing that he was left in charge of the store.

Dad gives me a "we'll talk later" nod but doesn't press me to answer as to why I'm standing in the living room of a broken-armed old lady and her ferocious dog, who is currently stuck to Ms. Gloria's side like glue.

For Gloria Crumb, he grins deep enough to show the dimple in his right cheek. "I'm Keith Logan, Annie's dad."

"Delighted to meet you," Gloria mutters in a way that means exactly the opposite. "Enchanted," she adds for good measure.

If I talked with that sour attitude, Dad would give me the sternest of looks. But with Gloria, he's sweet as a jelly doughnut.

"That looks like it hurts."

She scowls. *"Pish."*

He offers her a hand. "Let's get you on your feet."

"I can do it myself," she crabs at him.

The corners of my mouth turn up like they have a mind of their own. I have to admire the way she sticks to her grumpiness. JoJo would call it "gumption."

"Of course you can do it yourself," Dad says. He draws out all his vowels, really leaning in to his mountain accent. "But my mama would roll right over in her grave if I let you try."

She frowns and shakes her head, ready to argue. But as she reaches out to steady herself, her arm bumps the wall. She grimaces, clutching at it.

"All right," she says, like she's admitting defeat.

Dad scoops her up in one smooth motion. She looks like a doll in his arms. I was thinking he would set her on her feet—after all, her *legs* aren't broken—but instead he carries her out the door. Otto tries to follow, but the screen door snaps shut. He begins to bark and whine.

"Grab my purse," Gloria calls. "I know exactly how much money is in there, so don't get any grand ideas."

Yikes. The truth is, her gumption is a lot less enjoyable when she's aiming it at me.

"And lock the door," she shouts over Dad's shoulder. "Secure the perimeter. I don't need any vandals coming in!"

I do as I'm told. When I close the door on Otto, he starts to panic. I can hear him clawing at the wood.

Dad's settling Ms. Gloria in the front seat of his pickup, so I go around to get in behind Dad. She's telling him how she fell when she suddenly trails off.

"Wait," she says, brows furrowed. "Why were you at my door?"

I pause. If I say I was there to ring her doorbell and run away, I'm going to get in huge trouble with Dad. But as much as I am not a psychopath or a sycophant, I'm also no liar. I open my mouth, but somehow the words refuse to come out.

Dad glances at me and then back at Ms. Gloria. "Annie and her brother play at the park every day after school. Annie must have heard you calling for help."

I snap my mouth shut. Technically, it's true, even if it's not the whole story. I *did* hear her calling for help. It just so happens that the reason I heard her is because I was standing on the front porch at the time. Because I was the one who made Otto bark like a monster. Because I was the one who caused her to fall.

I wish I hadn't listened to Tyler. I wish I'd never even heard of Ding-Dong Ditch.

"My backpack," I say suddenly. "I left it at the park."

"We'll get it later," Dad says.

From inside the house, Otto chooses this moment to let out a deep howl. It's so loud, it makes my ears buzz.

Dad puts the truck in reverse and backs out of the driveway. "That's some kind of dog you have. What breed is he?"

This, it turns out, is exactly the right topic to take Gloria's mind off her situation. Gloria has long and mysterious, complex theories as to Otto's origin. In her mind, not only is he brave, brilliant, and loyal, he's also the most *handsome* dog ever.

My eyebrows practically pop off my forehead when I hear that. That dog is no kind of handsome I've ever known. I'm opening my mouth to say so when Dad catches my eye in the rearview mirror and winks. It's a good feeling, like we're on the same side. I wish I could enjoy it, but my insides are busy flip-flopping, imagining what he'll think when he finds out that it's my fault she's hurt.

We drive through the twisting mountain roads until we reach the hospital; then Dad helps Gloria get checked in. She's taken back quickly because of her advanced age. And possibly on account of her crankiness, although I keep that thought to myself.

Dad and I stay in the waiting room. After a while, a dark-haired man bursts through the door. He doesn't have a baby with him, but I recognize him from the picture on Gloria's phone.

I tug on Dad's sleeve. "That's Albert. He's here for Gloria."

Dad crosses the room. I watch as he explains. The man listens, then rushes over to me. He reaches out for my hand and starts shaking it briskly.

"I'm Albert," he says. "I can't thank you enough for saving Gloria. She's very lucky you were there."

I gulp, not saying a word.

Albert shakes Dad's hand as well. He's still saying *thank you* even as he turns to follow a nurse through the swinging double doors, on his way to Gloria.

When I look at Dad, he's beaming at me. For once, it's not Ray who is an excellent citizen. It's me.

I should be happy, but instead my heart sinks so low that it lodges somewhere around my ankles. Dad thinks I did the right thing with Gloria. He doesn't know that it's all the fault of me and my rotten luck.

CHAPTER
10

I barely sleep at night.

The covers twist around me like a tornado. Everything is too hot and too cold, too snug and too loose, too loud and too hushed. But even as I toss and turn, I know the truth.

Nothing is wrong with my room or my pajamas or the chirping crickets outside my window. It's me. *I'm* what's wrong. Each time I close my eyes, I replay the memory of what I did because Tyler dared me. How I walked up the driveway and reached the front steps. Otto's terrible bark. And the sickening *thud* of Gloria falling to the ground.

Way past midnight, I finally fall asleep. When I wake up, I go downstairs to the kitchen. Ray and Dad aren't there, but there's a note by the toaster.

Hey, Annie,
Ray and I went for a run. Come by the
store later today so we can talk about the
festival. Oatmeal's on the stove.
Dad

It figures that they went for a run—that's one more
way that Dad and Ray are alike. They're exercise fanat-
ics. Dad goes bonkers if he doesn't make his body work
hard for at least an hour a day. Last year, he broke his leg
and for six weeks was in a wheelchair the exact color of
a battleship. JoJo dropped off food for us every day, but
Dad was too miserable to enjoy it.

I ignore the oatmeal and rummage in the pantry until
I find my red box of Rainbow Puffs cereal. Dad calls it
my junk food. He says it's okay to eat as a snack sometimes, but I should never have it for breakfast because it
is not *the basis of a healthy meal*. I bet Ma would have let
me have a bowl every day without any trouble at all.

Before heading to the roof, I pour myself an extra-
big serving of Rainbow Puffs. I wait for my mountains to
make me feel better. When I try to draw them all my
lines look wrong. Even the Rainbow Puffs taste like sug-
ared cardboard.

I get dressed and put my bowl in the sink. The store
should be open now, so I decide to head downtown. But
I turn before I get to Dad's store, instead crossing over

the lake bridge to the park. I check the picnic table, but my backpack isn't where I left it. It probably got stolen. That would be just my luck.

I look at the woods across the street, knowing that Gloria's house is behind them. It has been less than a day since I was here, but it feels like a week has passed.

Something makes me go across the street to see the house. Before I make it to the front steps, I already hear Otto barking. There's a red SUV parked in the driveway. I try to think of what I would say if Gloria saw me. None of the words seems right.

As I'm standing there, trying to decide, the front door opens.

I hear a voice. "Easy, easy!"

The man from the waiting room backs onto the porch. He's pushing Otto inside, trying to close the door. It's Albert, with a sturdy, dark-haired baby strapped to his chest.

Finally, he manages to shut the door. He sighs.

"Hi," I say. "It's me, Annie. From the hospital."

Albert turns to look at me. His baby looks a lot like him, with thick, dark hair and pale skin. Albert uses hair product, but the baby's hair sticks out like dandelion fluff.

Albert blinks a few times like he's trying to place me. Then he nods. "You're the one who helped her."

Instead of answering, I wave at the baby. He doesn't wave back, but I don't take it personally. Not all babies are wavers.

"This is Fabian," Albert says, patting the baby's head. Fabian scowls at me from under his thick eyebrows.

I chew my lip. "Is she going to be okay?"

Albert sighs again. "They think so. They wanted to observe her overnight."

Relief floods my stomach. She's okay. For the first time since yesterday, I feel like I can breathe in all the way.

Albert steps off the porch. He cups his chin with his hand and surveys Gloria's house and yard. His eyes linger on the loose shutter, the overgrown weeds, the tilting wooden fence.

"I don't know how she thinks she can manage this place on her own," Albert says, almost to himself. "I've tried to tell her that she'd be better off in a place with people to help when she needs it. A place where she could have a little apartment and structured activities."

I don't know Gloria very well, but I know her well enough to understand that she'd only enjoy *structured activities* if she were the one doing the structuring. Maybe not even then. Besides, a little apartment would never fit all those cardboard boxes.

"That sounds like something she would hate," I say.

I make my tone as delicate as possible, but even so, Albert's eyes go round in surprise. He scratches his chin. "It's not ideal, but I don't know what else to do. At least she should consider getting rid of that horrid dog. There's no way she can manage him with a broken arm."

I shake my head. "That's a terrible idea. She may not be the nicest person in Oak Branch, but she doesn't deserve to have her dog taken away."

This time, my tone is less polite. Albert and I regard each other for a moment. Meanwhile, Fabian lets out a squawk, like I maybe surprised him, too. Albert drops a tiny kiss on the top of his little baby head.

As I watch, something inside me balls up tight. Balloons of questions float through my mind. Did Ma kiss *my* head to make me settle? Did I lean against *her* like that, sure she'd always be there?

It's easy to see what Gloria needs. If Albert weren't so busy with his baby, maybe he would notice.

"She needs someone to help her," I explain. "Someone who can check on her every day and feed Otto and let him go out to use the bathroom."

Albert brightens. "That's a wonderful idea."

I grin, pleased that he appreciates my explanation. "Thank you."

He scratches his chin again. "Do you think you could help?"

I gulp. "Oh. Hmmm."

But then I think of Gloria lying on the floor. How it's all my fault.

"Okay," I say. "I'll help."

There's a scrabbling from inside the house. We turn to look, and Otto is pressing his paws against the window.

It's like he knows he's being discussed and doesn't like it one bit.

Fabian's eyes are wide open. He pushes out his tiny lower lip as far as it will go. Albert gently bounces him up and down, but Fabian is not the type to be distracted by bouncing. He tilts his head back and wails.

My mouth drops open. I didn't know a little baby could make that kind of noise.

And then I hear, from inside, Otto letting loose with a howl of his own.

Albert removes Fabian from the carrier, saying, "It's okay, buddy. We'll go see Papa soon."

Fabian is not convinced. He weeps the entire time Albert is buckling him in the car seat. But when Albert hands him a toy giraffe, Fabian quiets just as suddenly as he began. Fabian looks at me with round, solemn eyes and jams the toy in his mouth.

Albert climbs in the front seat and rolls down the window. "I'll call your dad to work out the details. I'm thinking during the day would be best—I can check on her in the evening after work. Is that too much for you?"

"Yes!" I want to shout. "I take it all back."

But then I think: *I can handle a grumpy lady and a ferocious dog for a single day.*

"That's fine," I say. I paste a smile on my face. If Gloria could see me, she'd call me a "mealymouthed sycophant." She'd be right.

Through the open window, I can hear Fabian's giraffe squeaking as if it is dying a slow and painful death. Albert backs out of the driveway. When they're gone, I turn back to Gloria's house. Otto is standing there, staring at me. At least he's stopped howling. But when I think of his jagged teeth, I shudder. I don't know how I got myself into this mess. Tomorrow I'll be seeing those teeth up close again.

CHAPTER
11

Saturdays are the busiest days at the hardware store, but "busy" is a relative term. Over in Mountain Ring, Home-Made sees more customers in an hour than we do all day long.

Logan & Son is a good place, though. It smells of wood dust and fresh popcorn from the machine in the corner, free for anyone who wants a scoop. Grandpa Floyd built the gleaming wood shelves by hand, and not much has changed since he opened his doors for business.

When I go inside, the bells ring their greeting. Dad's in the corner fixing the key machine, which has been acting fussy. Ray's ringing up Mrs. Yang, who is buying clothespins, a ball of twine, and a small package of nails.

I get a pencil out of the jar by the register and use the sharpener on the wall to grind it into a perfect point. I'm ready to take notes. I wonder if we'll make it one big rosy maple moth that sparkles and shines in the sunlight. Or maybe we'll make dozens crawling on a giant hammer.

After he finishes at the key machine, Dad heads over to the checkout area. He squeezes my shoulder. "Albert called. Said you offered to check on Gloria every day while she's recovering."

My eyebrows pop up. "*Every* day?" I thought this was a onetime thing.

"Don't worry," Dad says. "I told him that Sundays we have church and you wouldn't be by until the afternoons."

"That's not what I . . . ," I start to say. But I break off when I see Dad's face. He's grinning wide—the grin he usually saves for Ray. My words trail away.

His eyes twinkle. "Real proud of you, Annie. Thought you wasted today drawing and daydreaming, but you went out of your way to be helpful and kind. I had no idea."

"Neither did I," I say.

He looks at me funny.

I clear my throat, thinking fast. "I mean, I didn't know if she would need me to come by twice in a day or just once."

Dad taps his chin thoughtfully. "I think he said that once would be fine, but maybe we should offer—"

"No!" I say, more sharply than I intend. "I mean, I wouldn't want to bother her."

I find my fake smile and paste it on again.

Dad nods as if it's settled. I guess it is.

"Let's talk about our plans for the float," Dad says. "Ray, why don't you pull out that sketch you made?"

Ray rummages under the register and emerges with a notebook. He spreads the pages on the counter. This is beyond a simple sketch. He must have spent a lot of time on it. He has all the measurements drawn out for the base, Dad's old trailer. He's drawn careful lettering that spells out *Logan & Son*.

My eyebrows squeeze into a straight line.

Ray glances at me.

"Just an idea to get us started," he says.

I look at his paper. "But this is so plain and boring." I don't mean it to be rude, just honest.

Ray hesitates.

I lean forward. "What about tying into the moth theme? Maybe we could add tissue paper or glitter or something eye-catching to get our message across?"

Ray stiffens. "This does get our message across."

Dad pulls a page closer to him. He's got to see my point. After all, this isn't a float—it's a sign on wheels.

"Not sure about that," Dad says. "The important thing is to get our name out there and demonstrate our old-fashioned, high-quality workmanship. Maybe we could create dovetail joints here on the side."

"Dovetail joints? No one is going to care about dove-tail joints during a parade," I say. "I was thinking we could experiment with glow-in-the-dark paint. Or maybe I could hook up some lights."

Dad shakes his head. "We don't want *showy*. That's why people go to places like HomeMade."

I scowl. "It's not showy. It's *creative*."

Ray taps his pencil. "Besides, the parade is during the day. There's no point in using special lights or glow paint during the *day*."

My face gets hot. This is reminding me of my disaster of a group project for Ms. Palumbo.

"Part of the event happens at *night*. Using lights would be unexpected—something that would draw people in—"

Dad rubs his chin. "Finishing touches. Little details. Right now we need the basics. Something solid and strong. We don't need anything newfangled."

Ray nods so fast, it reminds me of a yo-yo on a string. "That reminds me—I made a materials list."

He pulls out a list. I read the words "wallboard," "lumber," and "chicken wire" before my eyes glaze over and I almost die from boredom.

Dad, though, is excited. Within seconds, he and Ray are deep in conversation about bolts. *Bolts!* Who cares about bolts? They might as well be making a parade float of a giant bowl of oatmeal.

This project was supposed to make the three of us come together. But instead it's like our lopsided family triangle just got stretched out even further. This is a *Logan & Son* float. It's very clear that there's no room for *& Daughter*. They don't need me because they have it all figured out.

I knew I was right about group projects.

CHAPTER 12

Mornings, especially Sunday mornings, should not start with a pounding resembling a jackhammer. But that's exactly what's happening in the hall outside my bedroom door.

"Annie," Dad calls, rapping on the door. "Time to wake up!"

That's a lie—I'm sure of it. There's no way I could have possibly slept a whole night yet. My eyes are bleary and my tongue feels like it's covered in moss.

"Impossible," I mumble. "I need a do-over."

"Time for church," he says, in a singsong voice. He pushes the door open a crack.

I squint at my alarm clock. Seven thirty AM. Sunlight streams through my curtains. Early birds cheep loudly, like they've been awake and eating early worms for hours.

It feels like a dirty trick.

"In a minute," I say.

"Not in a minute. *Now*," Dad says. The sweet voice is gone. "We've got to get to church to set up the doughnuts and coffee for fellowship."

I sigh, giving my fluffy comforter a final squeeze. It is only the promise of powdered-sugar doughnuts that motivates me to launch myself out of bed.

Of course, when I do, I land right on the spiral edge of my sketchbook.

"Ouch!" I yell, rubbing my foot.

Dad's expression darkens. "No more dawdling."

"I'm not dawdling," I grumble. "My foot was practically impaled."

"Hurry," he says before closing my door.

I sigh, looking at my closet. I always hope some new clothes will magically appear in it, but they never do. I get dressed in church clothes and hobble downstairs.

Ray grins when he sees me. "Good morning."

Sometimes I simply cannot abide the fact that I'm related to people who are so aggressively cheerful in the morning. I glower at Ray to indicate that he has exceeded my tolerance for morning cheer.

I open the cupboard, even though I know I am out of Rainbow Puffs.

"There's fruit," Dad says. "And of course, there's oatmeal in the pot."

"I can't deal with oatmeal on a Sunday," I say. Scowling, I prod at the fruit bowl. I like bananas only when they're just barely yellow, and these are somewhere between brown and black. At the bottom of the heap, I locate a dusty-looking apple, which has no flavor when I bite into it. I hate it when an apple lets me down like that.

Riding to the church means a big conversation between Dad and Ray about the parade float. I stare out the window. They don't ask for my opinion and, for once, I do not offer it.

Dad pulls into the dirt parking lot of our church. The building is small and flat-roofed but friendly looking. Most of the families and young people go to a big church in Mountain Ring called Peak. They have an actual rock band and giant windows made of stained glass. They also have pastors who are much more dynamic than gentle, quiet Pastor Boone.

Today's sermon is about loving your neighbor. I choose to believe that this is a coincidence, not God trying to make me feel even guiltier. But the entire time, I think of Gloria and the sound of her scared voice asking for help. It's so different from how crabby she was once I saw her face-to-face. I wonder which is the real Gloria.

After church, we head over to JoJo & The Earl's for pancakes. JoJo grins when she sees me.

My stomach is already rumbling, this morning's apple and doughnuts a distant memory. "What's the special pancake today, JoJo?"

She winks. "Rhubarb pecan. Sound good?"

"Sounds like heaven on a plate," I say, handing her my menu.

"Buttermilk, please," says Ray. I shake my head. He always gets the same thing.

"I'll have my regular oatmeal, thank you," says Dad.

I wrinkle my nose. *Oatmeal*, when he could be eating JoJo's pancakes. In a million years, I'll never understand it.

"JoJo," Dad says, beaming. "Did you hear what happened with Gloria Crumb?"

My stomach tightens. "Dad. *Don't*."

"Annie saved the day," he announces.

JoJo's eyes widen. "Is that right?"

I feel sick. I don't want him telling the whole town. I'm the reason Gloria got hurt, and that's nothing to be proud of.

"Not exactly. What happened was—"

But Dad interrupts, waving away my words. "Let me brag on you a bit."

Then he tells the whole story—the whole story as he knows it, that is. That I was nearby and heard Gloria crying out for help. That she didn't want an ambulance, so I had the presence of mind to call Dad instead. With every word, his chest puffs out more. And with every puff of his chest, my stomach spins.

By the end of his explanation, he has a real audience—every single customer in the restaurant is listening, too.

When he finally wraps up with the part about my helping Gloria, he's grinning like he might burst. JoJo pulls a lace handkerchief from her pocket and dabs at her eye.

"That's so brave, sugar," she says to me. "I'm real proud of you."

I nod miserably. First Dad and now JoJo. There's no way I can let them down.

She pats my arm. "Come see me before you leave."

She moves along to help another table, and Ray and Dad return to their float-building discussion. I don't say much for the rest of breakfast. I push the rhubarb around on my plate and nibble at the edges of the toasted pecans. Nothing tastes right.

Before I leave, JoJo packs two big bags of food, fitting the containers inside with ruthless efficiency.

"I'm not sure she'll be able to manage all this," I say.

JoJo waves aside my protests. "She'll eat what she can. At least she'll have some options."

"Right," I say. "Options."

It must be nice to have them. I have no choice but to go along to Gloria's.

It's a warm afternoon and the air feels heavier than usual. Most of the time, my mountains give me comfort. But today, they make me feel like I can't escape.

The closer I get to Gloria's, the slower I walk. My legs feel like they're loaded full of rocks. I step onto the porch, shifting my body to adjust the heavy bags.

"Hello?" I say.

I'm answered by a loud bark two inches from me. I gasp and jump sideways—*clunk*. Somehow, I've managed to land one foot in an old clay pot. I kick at it wildly, and it splits into two with a *crack*.

The commotion makes Otto go bonkers—just my luck. I thought his bark was loud before, but now he sounds like he's being hunted by a rabid bear. Or, more realistically, like *he* is the one doing the hunting.

Between the pot, the noise, and the overstuffed bags in my arms, I struggle to keep my balance. I'm twirling like a deranged pinwheel and almost fall smack on my face. Finally, I pitch backward, elbows first, and crash into the window shutter, which comes loose in a groan. By some miracle, I do not drop JoJo's bags.

"What in tarnation," Gloria says. "What's all that racket?"

I kick the flowerpot pieces into the bushes. "Nothing!"

"Sure sounds like *something*," Gloria says back, her voice sharp and cutting.

I'll have to fix the shutter later.

"It's me, Annie Logan," I say over the barking. "I'm here to check on you."

There's a long pause. Otto quiets down.

"Go away," she finally says. "I don't need anyone fussing over me."

It's tempting. But when I think of Dad's face—how proud he was—I know I can't give up all that easily. Plus, what would I do with all this food?

"Albert asked me to check on you," I say. "To help take care of Otto."

Gloria mutters something that sounds like "pish." I wait for what seems like ages, but she doesn't say anything more. Otto switches from barks to high-pitched whining, like someone flipped the switch from *terrifying* to *annoying*.

A thought occurs to me.

"I have food," I say.

There's a long pause. Almost like he can understand me, Otto stops whining. He plops himself down at the screen door, panting.

Gloria clears her throat in a high-pitched, dainty way. "What kind?"

"Two big bags from JoJo and The Earl's," I say. "I've got barbecue—Eastern and Lexington."

"Eastern!" She sniffs. "I don't like that vinegar stuff."

She's deeply and irretrievably wrong about her taste in barbecue, but I choose not to comment.

"They also sent two types of slaw, collard greens, macaroni and cheese, and hush puppies," I say. "And an entire strawberry pie."

Gloria hesitates. "That's an awful lot to carry. Maybe you should bring it inside."

I ease myself through the screen door, praying that Otto won't choose this moment to switch into attack mode. He eyes me warily but stays silent. Like before, the house smells like soup and powdery breath mints.

Inside, the clutter is *extreme*. I didn't expect it to get *better* since I was here last, but I didn't think it would look worse. Albert should have tried to make a better path through the boxes. Gloria sits in a floral-patterned chair. The other chair, which matches, is piled high with newspapers. There's no couch or anywhere for people to sit. I guess she doesn't get many visitors.

With her good hand, Gloria readjusts the light blanket covering her lap. Today her hair is even wilder, like an electrified dandelion gone to seed.

She narrows her bright-blue eyes at me. "Kitchen's that way."

I walk in the direction she indicates, weaving through the piles of boxes and newspapers. The kitchen counters are stacked with dishes, open boxes of crackers, and cans of soup. A half-full bag of dog kibble leans against the toaster.

"Do you want me to make you a plate?" I ask Gloria, calling from the kitchen.

"Just a taste of everything," she says. "Except none of that vinegar barbecue!"

"Have it your way," I mutter under my breath.

"What was that?" she asks.

"Nothing," I call back to her. Gloria may be old, but her ears seem to work just fine.

I take out a plate from the cabinet, but it has crumbs and dried food stuck to it. All the plates in the cabinet are the same. I rinse one quickly and dry it with an ancient towel.

I make up a plate of samples of everything but the vinegar barbecue and then bring it to Gloria. Otto is lying on her feet. I carefully reach over him and try to hand her the plate, but she stops me.

"I can't hold it with my broken arm," she says crossly. "Put it on the tray."

I pull the ancient folding tray toward her chair and set it up. She tries everything, eating all of one item before moving to the next. She holds her fork in the air and peers at me.

"You're wearing a dress," she says.

I look down at myself, wishing I'd thought to grab my favorite green sweatshirt. I'm not much of a fan of dresses. Maybe I'd feel differently about them if they came with pockets and didn't always hike up in the back. This one is especially bad because it's scratchy and the exact color of cantaloupes.

"Church," I tell her—a one-word sentence that explains it all.

She shovels in another bite of slaw, then wipes her mouth daintily.

"That color is simply terrible on you," she says.

I wish again for my green sweatshirt. "Gee, *thanks*."

Even though I load my voice with as much sarcasm as I can muster, she doesn't seem to notice.

"With your coloring, you should try lavenders and blues," she continues.

I make a noise that sounds like *mmm* but really means, *Back off, Gloria Crumb.*

She's quiet, but it's not that she suddenly found her manners. It's more to do with the pile of delicious food she's managing to eat one-handed.

I squirm, itching my arm where the lace sleeve rubs.

Finally, she sets down her fork and wipes her mouth with a napkin. "Well, I am full as a tick."

If I were going to draw Gloria, I would need an extremely sharp pencil to do so. She doesn't have any soft lines about her. Her face is sharp and pinched like a pair of needle-nose pliers.

She squints at me. "Of course, now I'm thirsty."

"Oh," I say. "Do you want a glass of water?"

Gloria shakes her head. "A proper barbecue lunch calls for sweet tea. Tea bags are on the counter."

I believe it—it seems that every known object in the universe is on that counter.

"Yes, ma'am," I answer.

"I told you not to call me that," she says. "It's Gloria or nothing."

"Fine," I say.

"Pish," she says.

I've never met such a crabby person in my life. She's crabbing at me even as she's telling me to make her tea. I thought old ladies liked to make cookies and show pictures of their grandchildren.

I return to the kitchen. Finding something in this mess is going to be impossible. So much of the food is expired or moldy. I toss a half-empty container of pickles into the garbage.

"I hope you aren't throwing anything away!" Gloria shouts from the other room.

"Just organizing a little," I call back to her.

I eye a jar of grape jelly. I'm pretty sure it's older than I am. This time, I lower it gently into the trash can.

Eventually, I locate a box of tea. I return to the living room to show Gloria. Otto peers at me with one eye open, tongue hanging out the side of his mouth.

"I found the tea," I say.

Gloria adjusts the blanket around her. "Don't make it too sweet. I don't like it that way."

"No sugar," I say. That's great. It's one less thing I have to find in that mess.

Gloria rolls her eyes up at the ceiling. "I didn't say *un*sweet. I want *half*-sweet."

I hesitate. I've heard people order it that way at restaurants, but that doesn't mean I know how to make it. "And how would I do that?"

Gloria gives me a look like I'm a bug that crawled out from under the floor mat. "A girl who doesn't know how to make tea? Go on to the kitchen—I'll explain."

I want to ask why it's somehow worse to be a *girl* who can't make tea, but I hold my tongue. She's old and set in her ways. The only thing arguing will do is extend my time at her house, which is the last thing I want.

She barks out orders at me and I make the tea. First boil the water. Then add the sugar—she says five scoops. I have no idea what she means by a scoop, so I find a clean-ish serving spoon and use that. I stir the sugar until it's gone and then turn the heat on again. When I start seeing the first bubbles come up, I turn off the heat and add the tea bags.

This feels like it's taking a long time. I use the sugar spoon to push on the tea bags, trying to hurry things along a bit.

"Whatever you do," Gloria calls out, "never squeeze those tea bags. Makes the tea bitter."

I look down at the tea bags that I'm currently squishing.

"Of course not," I answer. Quickly, I add a few more scoops of sugar. That ought to hide the bitterness.

Then I put ice in a tall glass and pour until the glass is almost full. In the sunlight, it glows amber. I go back to the living room and put it on her tray.

She reaches for it, hand shaking, but manages to bring it to her lips. At first she looks pleased, but then she grimaces. "Somehow you made this too bitter and too sweet at the same time."

She sets it on the tray, then winces and rubs her arm. She's hurting. I wouldn't be in a good mood, either.

"Sorry," I tell her.

Gloria's eyes narrow. "Seventh-grade girl and can't make tea. I was doing a lot more than that by your age. Your mother should be taken to task!"

My cheeks burn. I don't see why she has to bring Ma into this.

"My ma isn't around," I say through clenched teeth. "But even if she were, I wouldn't care to learn. I don't see why I should learn to make tea when I don't even like it. I was trying to be nice!"

Gloria opens her mouth to say something more, but I don't want to hear it. The only thing stopping me from running out the front door is knowing that Dad would hear about it. Instead, I go to the kitchen and scrub the dirty dishes. Then I take out the trash. Finally, I return to the living room.

Otto is sprawled on his back, tongue hanging out the side of his mouth. His eyes are wide open and glassy-looking. I watch him for a long moment, but he doesn't blink. I look at Gloria.

"Is he okay?" I ask.

"He's sleeping," Gloria says sharply.

"But—his eyes are open," I say.

"So what?" she answers in a huff. "That's how he sleeps."

He snorts and rolls onto his side. His eyes are still open in a creepy kind of way. Like a very hairy zombie.

"Listen," says Gloria. "About the tea . . ."

I raise my eyebrows. Maybe she's going to apologize. "Yes?"

She nods crisply. "You'll get better tomorrow."

Right. *Tomorrow.*

Gloria gives me a sharp look. "Lock up on your way out."

I sigh and head for the door, shutting it tightly behind me.

This is going to be a very long, very unlucky summer.

CHAPTER 13

After supper, Dad, Ray, and I walk over to Lulu's for the town meeting about the festival. Somehow, the night air always feels more special up here in the mountains—it's sweet and crisp, like it comes direct from the stars themselves.

It seems like the whole town is crowded onto the patio at Lulu's. Twinkle lights strung around the arbor make the whole place glow.

"Hey there," says The Earl. He sits at a table with Mayor Barnes. The mayor's hair is the same shade of red as his son Tyler's, but instead of a buzz cut, the mayor wears it slicked back with lots of hair product. Dad and Ray pull up chairs and sit down. I stand to the side.

"It's an opportunity, that's what it is," says Mayor Barnes. "To bring in those tourism dollars Mountain Ring snatches away from us."

The Earl strokes his chin thoughtfully. "An opportunity to make our little town shine like it should."

Ray nods eagerly. "Mountain Ring isn't so great. What do they have that Oak Branch doesn't, anyway?"

I can't believe Ray, acting like a big shot. What does Mountain Ring have that we don't? For starters, Mountain Ring has two luxury ski resorts, a downtown with fancy shops and art galleries, and festivals almost every weekend. Plus, they're much bigger and have lots more choices for restaurants and shopping than we have in our little town.

The Earl claps Ray on the back. "Might want to avoid those direct comparisons, son. Comparing little Oak Branch to Mountain Ring is a fool's game."

The men's laughter booms. Ray's cheeks flush. I feel a pang for him, but he didn't think that idea all the way through.

I wander over to the long table set up with snacks and drinks, choosing a muffin and three cookies. I'm reaching for a napkin when I bump arms with someone. It's Faith.

"Hey," she says. She's holding a plate stacked high with treats. "I'm glad you're here. I have your backpack."

I frown. "My backpack?"

"Remember?" she says. "You left it the other day at the park. I brought it back here."

So that's where it went. I guess I should be glad it wasn't stolen, but mostly I'm confused.

"Why would you bring it *here*?" I ask.

She gives me a look. "I already told you. I'm staying with my aunt. This is her place—I'm working here this summer."

I smack my forehead. I get it now—Faith's aunt Louise is the same Louise who owns Lulu's. I don't know why I didn't make that connection. I've known Louise for years. She wears her locs gathered in a high ponytail and has big dimples when she smiles. She also has a habit of sneaking extra cookies in the bag whenever I visit.

"After I help set everything out, I'm going to stay for the meeting," Faith says. "Aunt Louise says I can work on her float. I'm going to make it look like a big coffee cup and paint those rosy maple moths on the side."

It must be nice to have someone excited about her float design. I wouldn't know what that's like.

"That sounds adorable," I say finally. "Maybe you could do dry ice to make the cup look like it's steaming."

After I say the words, I wish I could bite them back. This is Faith's project. She won't want me sticking my nose in.

But Faith nods like she's thinking it over. "Not a bad idea. Help me set these out, and then we can talk more about it."

I try to keep my mouth from dropping open. I said what I thought and she didn't get mad. We walk to and from the kitchen until the table is loaded with all kinds of treats.

Faith bumps my arm. "Let's go—everyone is at a table in the back."

I follow her, but when I see a flash of red hair, I stop walking.

"That's Tyler," I say flatly. The king of Ding-Dong Ditch, otherwise known as the king of Ruining My Summer. With my luck, of course he's here.

Faith looks puzzled. "Yeah, Tyler and a few others—Nailah, Alicia, Javier. Grant, too. Oak Branch Middle is offering service hours, so there are a lot of eighth graders."

I smile. "*Grant?* Just slipped that name in there at the end, huh?"

"Hush," she says, smacking me on the arm playfully.

I'm stuck. I want to spend more time with Faith, but the last thing I want is to be around Tyler.

When she sees me hesitating, she shakes her head. "Come sit with us."

I follow. When we get to the table, there are only two open seats. Somehow I end up taking the one next to Tyler. He has a stack of cookies in his hand: lemon poppyseed, white-chocolate macadamia, and chocolate cinnamon, and then he takes a bite of them all at the same time.

"There's no way that tastes good," I tell him.

He sees my expression. "What? You don't like cookies?"

"Not all together like that," I say. I take a small bite of my lemon poppyseed for emphasis.

Tyler smirks. "Sometimes I need maximum cookie infusion," he says.

I shake my head, and he laughs loudly. He sounds like a seal. I edge my chair away.

That doesn't stop him from leaning in my direction and talking in my ear. "What happened to you the other day when we were at the park? You were supposed to come back after Ding-Dong Ditch, not run away."

I open my mouth to tell him off. He thinks I ran away? Why would I do that? He has no idea of the consequences I'm facing. I'd love to see him washing Gloria's dishes and making her tea.

But I think better of it. If I tell Tyler, he will tell the whole world. Then everyone will know it was my fault she fell. I can't stand the idea of disappointing Dad like that.

"I had something else to do," I say in a "this conversation is over" tone.

He frowns and starts to say something else—but thankfully, JoJo starts calling for everyone's attention.

"Let's all settle down," JoJo says with a smile. "First, a few words from our mayor to start us off."

Mayor Barnes gets to his feet. He pauses for a moment, like he thinks there's going to be applause, but that's not realistic. He's not onstage—he's just a guy standing on a patio with muffin crumbs on his tie.

"I'm pleased to be here, talking about the future of Oak Branch," he says. "We need our town to be its own destination, not a little stop on the way to Mountain Ring."

JoJo pats her hair. "Our festival is named for the rosy maple moth. We picked it because it's a little something that's easy to miss. But when you look closer, you realize that it's quite special."

Mayor Barnes clears his throat. "First off: the festival will be held in four weeks."

This announcement starts a round of murmuring among the crowd. Four weeks doesn't seem like very much time.

"But that's so soon," someone calls out.

JoJo nods. "It's the only weekend this whole summer that Mountain Ring doesn't have a big event scheduled. We thought our little festival would stand more of a chance this way."

Discussion goes on. They're planning for a parade in the late afternoon, which will wind through downtown and end in the park near Gloria's house. Then, at the band shell, there will be food, music, and dancing. The whole time people are talking, Tyler gobbles cookies like it's his last day on Earth. I scoot my chair a little farther away.

They start splitting people into groups according to task. JoJo is helping coordinate the floats, Mayor Barnes is leading the music planning, and The Earl is planning all the food.

Grant looks at Tyler and Javier. *"Food."*

"Yes," says Javier.

"I'm going to do music," says Tyler, pushing his chair back. "Maybe my dad will let me DJ."

The boys get to their feet and head toward the food planning area. Grant glances at Faith like he thinks she'll go along.

She shrugs. "I'm doing floats."

"Me too," I say.

Faith and I head over to JoJo, who is busy writing a long list of planned floats.

"We'll use the old barn as building space for those who need it," says JoJo. The barn is on the back edge of downtown. It used to be part of an actual farm with animals, but now it's used mostly to store the town's holiday decorations.

JoJo bites her lip. "So many floats. I hope we aren't getting in over our heads."

I look around. Dad and Ray are deep in conversation. I'm grateful that I have Faith to talk to.

Her aunt Louise comes over to check on us. "How's it going, girls?"

Faith shows her the drawings, and I explain my idea for the dry ice.

She claps her hands together, eyes sparkling. "I love the detail y'all are putting in. This is going to be fabulous."

Faith grins. She and Louise have the same dimples.

Louise leaves to check in with the food committee, so Faith and I go back to looking at the sketch.

Faith frowns. "I wonder how to add the dry ice."

"Maybe the coffee cup could have a space inside to hold the dry ice, like a shelf along the rim. We could build it so the vapor can float around the cup." I hesitate, wondering if I shouldn't have said that *we* could build it. Faith might not want my help.

But she looks happy. "That's a great idea. So you'll help me? You won't be too busy with your family's float?"

"Absolutely," I say without hesitating. "I can help."

"Yes!" says Faith. She pulls out a pouch of colored pencils, and we start to sketch ideas for a design on the side of the coffee cup. Should it be a big rosy maple moth or lots of little ones? We decide to draw each idea and then make a decision.

I grab a yellow pencil and color in the moth's furry body. I hear Dad and look up. He's talking with Louise, using that same sweet-as-pie voice he used on Gloria, which is strange. Maybe he's making a habit of it. Ray is busy sketching. Neither of them glances over at me.

I look back at my sketchbook. Ray and Dad don't need me. I don't need them, either.

CHAPTER
14

The next day is sweltering. By the time I reach Gloria's porch, I'm covered in sweat.

"It's me," I say through the screen door. I brace myself for Otto's barking, but for once he's quiet.

"Come on in," she says crankily. "Do you need an engraved invitation?"

She doesn't have to be so grumpy all the time. *Maybe she wouldn't be if my bad luck had never showed up on her doorstep*, I think, but I quickly push the thought away. I let the door snap shut behind me. Inside, it smells even more like soup than usual.

There's a fan blowing in the front room. Albert must have set it up when he checked on her last night.

I head to the kitchen and refill Otto's food and water dishes. The room looks better now that I've tidied it. I wonder if there's anything else I could do. My mind replays the sound of her falling, that sickening *thud*. If she fell again when her arm was healing, it could be really bad.

I return to Gloria. "Should I sort through some of these boxes for you? Since I'm here anyway, I mean."

She peers at me suspiciously. "You sound like you've been talking to Albert. Last night he told me I should get rid of it all so I can move to Shady Lane with all the riffraff."

That's the name of the old folks' place on the outskirts of town. We did a fourth-grade service project there, making art for the residents.

"I've been there," I say. "The people who worked there seemed nice."

She smacks her good hand against the arm of the recliner. "They can carry me out of this house when I'm dead and not a moment before!"

Then she quiets, reaching down to trace her fingers through Otto's hair, the part on top of his head where it sticks straight up. She rubs his ears, and his eyes shut. He's completely blissed out.

"Even if they *are* nice, that's not the issue," she says finally. "Otto couldn't go with me. No dogs allowed."

She continues to stroke his ears. Gloria may have harsh edges and sharp corners with most of the world. But with Otto, she's as gentle as a blurred pencil line. Which Gloria is the real one? Crisp and mean or soft and kind?

We're quiet like that for a while. Otto sighs. To Gloria, Otto is beautiful. Without him, her whole life would fall apart.

"I'll leave the boxes where they are," I tell her.

She looks startled, like she forgot I was there. "No, no. It was a good idea. It would be one less thing for Albert to fret over."

"I could organize them a little," I say. "Show you what I find and you can decide."

"*Pish,*" she says. "Most of it's junk—the kind that accumulates over a lifetime."

I want to argue, but after seeing what she's kept in her kitchen, it's hard to be very confident. It probably *is* junk—a whole *lot* of junk. But at least it will give me something to do.

She looks at me warily. "Don't think you'll find anything expensive. I don't have antiques or anything collectible. There's nothing worth stealing."

Stealing! That does it. It's one thing to be crabby. It's another thing entirely to accuse me of being a thief.

My face burns. "I'm not going to steal your stuff."

"Hmph," Gloria retorts. "*Pish.*"

I grit my teeth. "Look, if you don't want me to help, say so. I'll fill Otto's dishes and then leave. I don't care about your boxes. I don't even care if you fall and break your other arm."

I gulp, realizing that I've gone too far. It isn't even true. But she should know that I'm not a thief.

Gloria glares at me. All her soft lines are gone. "I thought little girls were supposed to be *sweet*."

My breath catches in my throat. So she thinks I'm not sweet, when I visit every day without complaining even *once*? When I do her dishes and bring her food—when I take care of her terrifying dog? I'll show her what "not sweet" looks like.

I put my hands on my hips and glare right back at her. "I thought old ladies were supposed to be *gentle*."

She scowls. "Girls should be sugar and spice and all things nice!"

I stomp my foot. "Old ladies should be baking cookies. And knitting those little shoes for babies!"

We stare at each other for a moment. I'm breathing hard. Her eyes glint like sharpened steel.

"Booties," she says, spitting out the word.

My mind whirls. Is this like her saying *hand phone* for *cell phone*?

"What are you talking about?" I ask.

"*Booties*," she says. "The knitted shoes for babies."

"Whatever!" I bellow.

At first, I think she's going to shout at me. But instead, she tips her head back and cackles. She laughs and laughs, like she will never stop. But eventually she does.

She wipes her eyes with a tissue. "All right, Annie P. Logan. If you say so."

I stomp over to the door. As I do, I hear her mutter, "Baking cookies," which sets her off into peals of giggles. I close the door firmly behind me.

I don't know why I offered to help. I don't know why she laughed so hard. I don't know who the real Gloria is, and I don't care one bit.

CHAPTER
15

Painting without good light is not really recommended. But the only time Dad is free to paint the band shell is after the store closes. So that's why Dad, Ray, and I are painting at night.

Actually, I'm not even painting. Lucky Ray is using the roller. He's happy, whistling as he works. All I get to do is hold the ladder for Dad.

"It's hot," I say. "It's *miserable*. Can we come back on a different day?"

Ray stops whistling. "At least it's not raining."

"We have to finish before the festival," Dad says. "You know that."

I shrug, wiping the sweat from my forehead.

"Annie!" Dad barks. "Keep the ladder steady."

"There should be a better way to do this," says Ray.

Dad's lips press together in a line. It's quiet except for the squicking sound of the paint rollers.

"If we had some scaffolding or something to stand on, we wouldn't need ladders," Ray points out.

"This will have to do," Dad says shortly.

We're all quiet for a while. I wish Ray and Dad believed in decent conversation. Or at least a radio.

Ray clears his throat. "Dad, have you given any thought to my idea?"

Dad frowns but keeps rolling paint. "About the maker space?"

I'm tired of being left out of all the important discussions. "What are you talking about?"

Ray brightens. "Maker spaces are getting really popular—areas with tools and materials so kids can build things. I was thinking we could start a service at Logan and Son where we design them."

"I don't think we're in a position to expand right now," Dad says distractedly.

"It would be a great way to bring business to the store," Ray adds. I roll my eyes. My brother, the future businessman.

"Not now, son. Get back to painting," Dad says. This time, his tone is gruff.

Ray's shoulders slump. Dad usually takes Ray seriously, and he never uses that tone. For once, Ray gets a little taste of how it is for me, and he doesn't like it one bit.

"Coming down," Dad says.

I hold the ladder until he is standing on the ground again.

He sets down the roller and crosses to Ray. "I promise we can talk about it later. With the festival and everything else, I'm too busy to add another thing to my plate."

Ray sticks out his chin. "But it would bring in money. You don't have to do anything. I'll do it all—"

Dad sighs. "It's not that simple, son."

"Speaking of the festival," I say. "I've been thinking a lot about our float—"

Dad's forehead creases. "Not now, Annie. We need to focus on painting, if you think you can manage holding the ladder steady for me."

I've had about enough. First I had to deal with grumpy Gloria. Now I have to deal with grumpy Dad.

I cross my arms. "I don't want to hold the ladder. I want to paint."

Dad takes a deep breath and lets it out slowly. "We'll finish faster this way."

I kick at the ground. "It isn't fair. I'm really good at painting. Why can't I help?"

Dad frowns. "This isn't the same as painting your pictures, Annie. This is important."

My eyebrows pop up in disbelief. "Dad! My art is *super* important!"

Dad winces. "You know what I mean."

"No one in this family understands me!" I'm yelling now. I want him to hear me. I want him to *notice*. I wave my arms like I'm drawing an enormous exclamation point in the sky. My arm bumps into something, but it isn't until I see Dad's face that I realize what I've done.

"Annie! No!" he yells.

It happens in slow motion—my arm hits the paint tray in just the right spot, the paint arcing through the air, the roller hitting me in the head. The paint dripping thickly down my forehead. It coats my hair and runs into my eyes.

"I can't see," I say.

Dad picks up a clean rag and hands it to me. I wipe my face.

"Did you get it in your eyes?" Dad asks.

My eyes are watering. I'm not sure if it's the paint or because I messed up again.

"I couldn't help it," I say.

Dad sighs, rubbing his temples like he has a headache coming on. He looks at the spilled paint, and it's like I can see him calculating the extra work it will take to clean up my mess. I always manage to ruin everything.

"You look like you had a fistfight with a vanilla milkshake," Ray says.

I stomp my foot. "You be quiet, Ray."

He snickers and goes back to painting.

Dad looks at me carefully. "Go on home and flush your eyes out with water. Ray and I will finish up."

Ray turns around, bug-eyed. "Really? It's just a little paint and she gets—"

Dad sends him a pointed look. Ray turns back around.

Guilt pangs in my heart, but I ignore it. I want to go home and wash off this mess. I want my roof. I want my sketchbook. I want to be alone.

PART THREE

A Life in Boxes
From the Collected Drawings of Annie P. Logan
Dimensions: 8" × 11"

CHAPTER
16

The next day, after taking care of Otto, I get started on Gloria's boxes.

The first box is full of paper—mostly ancient receipts and bank statements. I plan to ask Dad if they need to be shredded or if they're too old to matter.

The second box is a tangle of Christmas lights. I plug in the strands, but most of them don't work. One flickers to life, but I swear I smell something burning. I throw them away.

The third box is empty except for crumpled tissue paper. Maybe someone meant to throw it away and never got around to it.

The room is already looking better with less stuff in it, and it has to be safer for Gloria. I'll open another—the large one that sticks out into one of the aisles. Even though it's big, it's loosely packed. As I slide it toward me, the contents shift and I hear a metallic *clang*.

When I open the box, I gasp. Inside are pictures—some loose and some framed. Programs and ticket stubs. She'll want to keep these; I know it.

There's a rubber-banded stack of school pictures starting in kindergarten and going all the way up. "This is Albert, right?"

"That's him. Started babysitting him when he was small. Now he thinks he's my babysitter, with the way he checks on me all the time," she grumbles.

Gloria as a *babysitter*? I guess I assumed Albert was her nephew or something. I can't imagine someone paying Gloria actual money to take care of her kid. I wonder if she was friendlier back then.

I find an old photograph. Six kids standing on a sidewalk in front of some trees. The oldest, a girl, holds a baby on her hip. The boys are in a line next to her, from tallest to shortest. I can't tell how old the baby is. Older than Fabian, I think, but not by much.

I hold up the picture. "What about these kids?"

Gloria glances at it and then looks away. "That's me."

I feel my eyes bug out. "This is *you*?"

"Oldest of seven," she says grimly. "Daddy was a mean drunk, and Mother wore herself to the bone trying to make ends meet. I raised that crew the best I could."

I study the picture. The boys' clothes are patched and faded, but shirts are tucked in and hair is neatly combed.

"And the baby?" I ask.

Her eyes twinkle. "Julia. Fat and happy, like a baby should be. Doctors said she *wasn't quite right*, which was both unkind and inaccurate. To me, she was perfect. A friend to everyone—the best of the bunch."

"Where is she now?"

Gloria's smile fades. "She died in childhood. Her heart."

"Bad luck," I say quietly.

Gloria's frown deepens, but she doesn't answer.

"What about your own kids?" I know I'm being nosy, but I can't help it.

"*Pish,*" Gloria says, shaking her head. "Never married."

Oh. Maybe that's why she's so lonely now.

"Wipe that look off your face," she says, scowling. "I had plenty of offers! But I never had much use for a man, or for children after raising all those wild boys."

I must look doubtful. She clicks her tongue when she sees my expression.

"There's more than one way to make a life," she says.

I hold up a framed photo showing a woman and a boy on a Ferris wheel, wearing matching T-shirts that say *Gingerbread Island*. Their grins are wide.

She peers at the photograph, smiling when she realizes what it is. "We were at the old fun park. Albert used to love the coasty rollers."

"Coasty rollers?" I ask. "Do you mean roller coasters?"

"That's what I said!" she says angrily, turning back to the television. "I told you I don't need to see these!"

My cheeks burn. I place the picture back in the box, packing it carefully so it doesn't fall over. It doesn't seem right to throw these things away.

Otto is lying at Gloria's feet and is shaking a little. I can't tell if he's scared or just old, like Gloria. But when he looks at me with sad eyes, I feel bad for him, like I feel bad for Gloria. Us bad-luck people have to stick together.

"I thought I was supposed to be taking Otto out for exercise," I say. "Does he ever need to go out on a walk?"

Gloria frowns. "He doesn't like to go out front. Won't leave that porch. I let him out in the back when he needs it."

"I'll take him out back," I say. "Maybe he would want to run around a little bit."

"Suit yourself," Gloria says, turning back to the television.

"Come on, Otto. Want to go out? It's nice outside. Do you want some fresh air?" I try to ask him in all kinds of ways, but he ignores me like I'm smaller than a flea.

Gloria glowers at me. "You're too timid. You have to tell him what you're doing. Tell him with confidence."

I look at his teeth and hesitate. He doesn't exactly scare me anymore, but I don't feel all that confident.

"Otto!" Gloria says. "Outside!"

Otto springs to his feet and bounds for the door. Now that he's been convinced to go out in the world, he's like a different dog. I follow behind to see what he'll do. But the second my foot lands in the yard, it skids. I've stepped right in a pile of dog poop.

I glare at him. "Really, Otto?"

He runs over and grins at me like he's proud.

"Disgusting," I tell him. He licks me on the shin.

I reach down to rub his ears. "I know what I'll be doing this afternoon, Otto. Cleaning up your gigantic mess."

I find rubber gloves and trash bags under the kitchen sink. Otto and I spend most of the afternoon outside while I clean up his messes.

He sniffs at my ankles for a while, then chooses to lie in a sunny patch in the yard where he can fully supervise what I'm doing. Every so often, he whines a little. Then he gets up, heads back to the sliding glass door, and peeks in for a spell. Eventually, he settles himself among the tall blades of grass, tail wagging.

"You're a strange dog," I tell him. He rolls on his back in the grass.

When I finish, I make a trip to the garbage cans outside Gloria's garage, then wheel the can out to the curb. Back inside, I triple-scrub my hands and let Otto back inside. He trots over to Gloria and sprawls out at her feet.

Gloria looks at him and sniffs the air. "He smells."

Poor Otto. It's true that he has a distinct odor—a peculiar mixture of Fritos, dirt, and wet towels—but it isn't his fault. I can't imagine that he's had a bath in recent memory.

"Well, your yard smells a million times better now," I say. "So at least there's that."

She ignores me, pulling the blanket around her. Otto gazes at Gloria, tail thumping. Suddenly, I understand what all those trips to the sliding glass door were about.

"He kept checking on you," I say, realizing that it's true. "He wanted to make sure you were okay."

"Is that right?" Faint traces of a smile appear, like a beam of sunlight trying to break through on a cloudy day. Her face is like the girl in the photograph, standing on the street holding the baby. She might be tired and grumpy, but she also looks proud.

Gloria reaches for Otto, but he's just out of reach. From the way she winces, I can tell it hurts her to stretch.

I go to them. "Come on, Otto. Stand up." I brush off the blade of grass that's stuck to the top of his head.

He clambers to his feet and leans against Gloria, tail wagging fast.

Gloria rubs behind his ears. "Don't you worry. I'll never, ever leave you behind."

There's more than one way to make a life. There's more than one way to make a family.

Otto looks at me, pink tongue hanging at a jaunty angle. *Don't worry, Otto. I won't do anything that would take you away from her.*

I swear he almost winks.

CHAPTER 17

I never stopped to consider the idea that cleaning up poop might improve a relationship. If I had known, maybe I would have tried it before. But after that day, things are different between Otto and me.

As the week goes on, he doesn't bark at me once. He seems to look forward to our time in the yard. I find a dog brush in one of Gloria's cabinets, and he lets me loosen his tangles. By the time I'm done, his coat is shining.

Then he actually chases a squirrel across the grass. I tell him he is very brave, and Otto looks pleased with himself. For one quick second, I think he is almost a little bit cute.

Almost.

When I go up to Gloria's door, I let myself in like usual. Today she's on the phone. Her voice sounds pinched and worried. Otto follows me to the kitchen as I refill his water bowl.

"You must be hungry today," I say. I add the kibble to his bowl and he starts chomping.

"Annie! Fetch me my purse from the hall closet," Gloria calls.

I open the door and peer inside. It's crowded with all kinds of stuff but no purse.

I go back to the living room. "It's not there."

Gloria clutches the phone in one hand. Even from across the room, I can hear a voice squawking on the other end of the line.

"Oh no. Oh no, oh no, *oh no*," Gloria says. Her eyes shine for a moment; then fat tears roll down her cheeks.

Now I'm completely confused. Why would someone be yelling at Gloria?

She covers the receiver so he can't hear her talk. "This man is very angry with me," she whispers. "Can you talk to him?"

I frown but take the phone. "Hello?"

"I need that credit card!" He's shouting.

I scrunch up my forehead. "A credit card? Why do you need that?"

The voice on the line growls in frustration. "As I've already explained, I am with the government and the bank, and if you don't give me a credit card and social security number right now, we will take your car!"

A knot forms in my stomach. He's talking so fast, I can barely understand his words. Gloria, next to me, is weeping.

Something about what he's saying seems wrong, but I can't put my finger on it. I try to think through his words. "The government *and* the bank? Shouldn't you already have those numbers, then?"

"We will take your car away today," he shouts.

Gloria hears him shout and almost jumps out of her seat. I can see the fear on her face.

But it makes me suspicious. I can't say for sure about the government, but I do know the people at Oak Branch Bank would never yell at anyone. This doesn't seem right.

"Let me get a pencil and I'll write down your number," I say, thinking fast. "My dad will call you back."

There's a long pause on the line and then a *click*.

I look at Gloria. "He hung up."

"He said he was going to take my car," Gloria sobs.

Her car—I think about the empty driveway. I think about the empty garage.

I bite my lip. "But, Gloria. You don't *have* a car."

Her eyes widen. We are quiet for a long time.

Finally, she looks up. "Why did he call me?"

"He wasn't very nice," I tell her. "I think he was trying to trick you and take your money."

Gloria nods somberly. "I was remembering a different car I used to have. A big Buick with huge doors. Albert called it the Blue Magoo." Her eyes are wide, and they don't look fierce at all.

"Everyone gets mixed-up sometimes," I tell her.

Her cheeks are still wet from crying. Suddenly, she looks very small and alone, sitting in her chair. Otto's tail wags, and he nudges her legs. She reaches to pet him distractedly.

"Maybe we should call Albert," I say. "He might know what to do."

"No," she says. Her voice is soft, especially for Gloria.

"But . . ."

I watch her, running her hands over Otto's hair. His tail wags gently. Gloria isn't crying anymore. Her gaze on Otto is bright and alert. He has that effect on her.

"Albert would pack my bags if he knew," she says simply.

"I don't know—"

"*Please.* Otto needs me. I need him, too."

He's like her baby. The thought hits me in a flash. Once I think of it that way, I know I'll never tell. I couldn't bear separating them.

I sigh. "Fine. But I'm going to program your phone so these unidentified numbers can't call you."

"Fine," she says. And then, after a moment: "Thanks."

It's barely above a whisper. My eyes widen, but she isn't looking at me—she's rubbing Otto's ears. Otto, for his part, looks like he's floating on a cloud of happiness.

I set the phone down. "I'll make tea. Then we can do a few boxes."

She nods. I make the tea and let Otto out. I've given up on getting the tea right. I've noticed she always seems to drink it, even though I supposedly make it wrong. So now when she says "too sweet!" I pretend I didn't hear her.

She drinks her tea, even though she grumbles a bit. Eventually, she seems to feel better. Sometimes she seems easily confused and sometimes she's very clear. I don't understand why.

I peeked in this box the other day but decided to save it for later. It's stacked full of old photographs. Right on top is a picture of a young woman in a uniform with a scarf knotted at her neck. She looks extremely glamorous. When I hold it up to show Gloria, she smiles.

"Let me see those," she says. She sorts through the stack, looking at the pictures one by one. I try to be patient, but my curiosity is wiggling around and trying to get out. Over Gloria's shoulder, I see the woman at the Eiffel Tower, on the peaks of mountains, standing at the base of waterfalls, and even at the pyramids in Egypt.

There's something familiar about the young woman, the way she squints at the camera.

"Gloria," I breathe. "Is this *you?*"

"I was a flight attendant after Julia died," she says. "*Stewardess*, they said back then."

My eyes widen. I never thought of Gloria anywhere else but this little house on this little street in this little town.

She sees my face and laughs. "Thought I'd stayed in Oak Branch my whole life? Not a chance. I could see the writing on the wall."

I frown. "The writing on the wall—what does that mean?"

Gloria rolls her eyes. "Again, what *do* they teach children these days? It's an expression. It means that I could see the way that things would play out if I stayed. There weren't many choices for girls in those days. Get married or be a teacher or nurse. Not for me—I wanted to write my own story."

I shake my head slowly. "I've never even been on an airplane," I tell her.

Her eyes sparkle. "Neither had I. Trust me when I say it didn't matter where I came from. What mattered was where I was going."

"Wow," I say. "I can't really imagine leaving Oak Branch."

Her eyebrows frown into a line. "Whyever not?"

"Well—" I say, then stop. I guess I don't know why.

Gloria taps her fingers against the arm of the chair, waiting for an answer.

"Because of Dad and Ray," I say slowly. "And because of my mountains—I love them."

"Pish," says Gloria.

I sigh. "What do you mean, *pish?*"

"Pish!" she crows. "My dear girl, have you ever considered there is no shortage of mountains to climb?"

She digs in the box until she finds what she's looking for—a photo of a woman on a mule, a spectacular view surrounding them.

"Is that you?" I squeal.

"At the Grand Canyon," she says proudly. "All by myself, might I add. It was thrilling—terrifying but thrilling. But I was doing exactly what I wanted. That's the benefit of listening to the true longings of your heart."

I frown, thinking.

Gloria looks at me carefully. "What's the longing of your heart, Annie?"

"Having Ma come back home," I say automatically.

"Ah," says Gloria. She sounds almost disappointed.

"I know she left," I explain. "But she's the only one who understood me—the only one who would understand me now. She always told me I was born under an unlucky star. She knows that I don't mean to cause bad things; I can't help it."

Gloria hands me the stack of pictures, and I put them back in the box.

We're both quiet for a moment, and then I can't take it anymore.

"What is it?" I ask. "I can tell you want to say it."

132

Gloria rearranges herself on the chair, doing her best to sit up straight. I try not to roll my eyes. It seems like she has a speech she's been waiting to say.

She makes a little *ahem* noise, clearing her throat. "I understand you've had your share of disappointments. Maybe that's where you're from, but it doesn't mean a thing about where you're going."

I scowl. "That's easy for you to say. I have no idea where I'm going."

"Pish," she says. "I have a feeling it has something to do with that sketchbook pad you drag along with you everywhere." She smiles like she's pleased with herself.

I shift uncomfortably. I don't want to talk about my art with Gloria.

"Anyway," I say in a change-the-subject kind of way. "Why did you stop being a flight attendant?"

Her expression fades a bit. "My mother was dying. All my brothers were busy with their lives, so I moved back to Oak Branch to take care of her."

"That's not fair, about your brothers!" I say. But inside I think, *Maybe Gloria is unlucky like me.*

She's still looking at the photos in her lap.

"Sounds like rotten luck," I try again.

She shakes her head. "Not luck. Just life."

Disappointment crashes inside me. I thought for a moment that Gloria and I were the same. Not the crabby Gloria, not the scared Gloria, but the real one deep inside.

"It isn't fair," I tell her. "You worked so hard for your brothers. And then you had a job you loved but had to stop to take care of your mom."

She sighs. "If you want to see it that way, I suppose. But who gets to say which parts are lucky? Lucky that I got the job of my dreams or unlucky that I had to give it up? Lucky that I had a sister like Julia or unlucky that she died young?"

I open my mouth to argue. For me, life and luck are twisted together.

"You can't pick and choose, Annie. Life is a mix of good and bad. Things have a way of evening out."

Not luck. Just life.

Maybe that's true for Gloria, but it's not that way for me. I believe in luck, even if she doesn't. I believe in it, like Ma always said.

I open my mouth to speak, but Gloria is shaking her head.

"I'm worn out," she says. "You go on and go now. I'll see you tomorrow."

She nods like it's decided. I guess it is. I move the box of photographs out of the way so she won't trip. I scratch Otto behind his ears. Then I shut the door behind me.

CHAPTER
18

When I leave Gloria's, I head for the barn. I'm the only one here, so I switch on The Earl's radio.

It's set to a country station, one of the few that we receive here in the mountains. The song is about being laid low by heartbreak. The music is smooth and easy, but the voice is on the rough side, like the singer's been down one too many dusty roads. It's a great combination—a perfect song for an afternoon in the barn.

I make a beeline to JoJo and The Earl's float anyway—unlike Ray and Dad, *they* appreciate my help. Besides, JoJo is paying me in pie.

Their float has an oversize version of that split-down-the-middle table in their restaurant, and it needs a tablecloth. I grab my paints and get to work.

Filling in the yellow squares is calming, and I sink into the task like it's what I was born to do. The barn's wide-open doors allow me a glimpse of green trees whenever I choose to look up. And even when I don't look up, the mountains send me breezes that smell like pine trees and sunshine. No matter what, my mountains know where to find me—how to remind me that they'll always be there.

I'm so absorbed in the task that I don't notice anyone coming into the barn.

"Hey," Ray says from right behind me.

Startled, I jump in the air, sloshing paint from the container. Of course, with my luck, some of it splashes across the tablecloth's tidy yellow squares.

"Ray!" I shout. "Don't surprise me like that."

"I didn't mean to," he says. He grabs a roll of paper towels and helps me dab the cloth.

"Quit smearing it," I say. "Why are you here anyway?"

"Dad has a meeting at Lulu's tonight. He said we should do Friday night dinner ourselves," he says.

"Weird," I say. We always go to JoJo & The Earl's as a family.

Ray shrugs. "Festival stuff, I guess."

That must be it. With the big event only three weeks away, everyone in our town is turned upside down.

Thankfully, we're able to scrape off most of the spilled paint.

"I wanted to finish tonight," I tell him. "But I'm not even halfway there."

He looks at me sideways. "Do you want my help?"

My first thought is, *Absolutely not*. I don't want him to think I need him in any way, shape, or form. And shouldn't he be working on the Logan & Son float anyway?

But this float is for JoJo and The Earl, and something tells me they'd want me to say yes. Besides, this table-cloth is plenty big.

I tilt my head toward the paints. "You can work on the red half if you want."

He holds up a container. "This one?"

I nod, and he picks a brush that's similar to mine. We each sit cross-legged on the base of the float, fill-ing in our squares. Ray whistles along quietly with the radio.

When I take a break to stretch my fingers, I look at what he's done so far. I didn't expect him to be so quick—he's almost caught up to me. His squares are nice and crisp, too.

"You're good at making edges," I tell him.

The corner of his mouth quirks in a half smile. "I've had some practice painting lately. Guess it's not all that different."

The band shell. I watch Ray, waiting for a comment about the huge mess I made—or to tell me how I should have helped more that day. But he doesn't say a thing, just goes back to whistling.

Thinking about painting makes me think of other things that could use a coat or two. Like Gloria's front door. Gloria's shutters. Gloria's pretty much *everything*.

"Ray, Gloria's house needs paint. The only problem is that I don't think Gloria has much money. If she did, things probably wouldn't be so run-down in the first place."

Ray's eyebrows furrow together. I can tell he's thinking, but he waits to finish the square he's working on before looking up.

"We could use Oops Paint," he says.

Oops Paint isn't a real brand of paint. It's what happens when someone makes a mistake while mixing (*"oops!"*) or if a customer asks for a specific color but then after it's mixed, they decide they don't like it. For example, our downstairs bathroom is painted in Oops Paint—an unfortunate yellow that would give a rubber duck a run for its money.

It's not exactly fair for someone to change their mind after it's mixed, because the store loses money. But Dad says it's better than losing a customer to HomeMade.

Ray leans back on his heels. "I'm helping Dad in the store tomorrow, but I could come over Sunday after church."

My brother may annoy me sometimes, but he also knows how to help. Sometimes there's an upside to practical and predictable.

Ray goes back to his work, whistling along to the radio. Together, we work until the sky turns a quiet pink. Then we lock up the barn and get our orders from JoJo and The Earl's to go. We carry the warm bags with us and take the long way home.

CHAPTER
19

It's Saturday, and I am free.

Yesterday Albert messaged Dad, saying that he and Fabian would spend the day with Gloria. Dad didn't need me at the store, so I'm helping with floats.

The barn bustles with activity. Already today I've painted cardboard bookshelves for Oak Branch Books, cut foam vegetables for Quinn's Market, and glued tissue paper to the lake for the town council float.

"Thanks so much for helping out," everyone says.

No one asks why the Logan & Son float isn't further along. The trailer is pushed up along the side of the wall and looks downright abandoned. I'm staying out of it. If Ray and Dad want help, they can be the ones to ask.

Right now, Faith and I are wrangling a roll of chicken wire. Together we stretch, bend, and shape it. Making the curved edges of the coffee cup is a real challenge, and we haven't even started the handle yet.

"Got it?" Faith asks.

"Hold it closer together if you can," I say. Faith pushes the wire together, and I anchor sections using zip ties.

I have learned that Faith has a brain for building things. I know how to come up with ideas that look good, but she has a way of figuring out how to put them together.

She is also a master of teamwork. I suggested blue for the mug and she wanted green. But unlike certain group projects on ancient Greece, we managed to work out our different opinions. She suggested we mix up the colors we like best and then show Louise and let her pick. Of all the colors we mixed, Louise picked the one right in the middle. So the Lulu's mug will be turquoise—the exact color of Tahitian Breeze. Both blue and green, better together.

Later this week, we'll do papier-mâché, dipping long strips of newspaper in starch before laying them across the wire form. After they dry, the surface will be smooth and paintable. That's the plan anyway.

Even though I love art, I admit that I don't always like starting. It can be overwhelming to see a project that is all potential, when no real decisions have been made. But right now, we're in the sweet spot where everything is coming together. There's still plenty of work to do, but it's easy to see the path ahead. This is my favorite part.

I should be happy. I am happy. And I thought I'd be so relieved to have a day without Gloria and Otto. But even though I'm loving where we are with this project, my thoughts keep sliding sideways over to that funny-looking dog and that grumpy old lady. I wonder if Otto gets nervous when baby Fabian fusses. I wonder if Gloria is sharing the last of the strawberry pie. I wonder if Albert will notice that I've moved boxes to the garage.

"Ouch!" I say, pulling my hand back from the roll of chicken wire Faith and I are unrolling. The metal edges of the wire are unforgiving.

Faith startles. "Did it pinch you? Are you okay?"

I squeeze my finger. "It's okay—a little bad luck, as usual."

Faith's forehead wrinkles. "What do you mean, *as usual*?"

My cheeks get hot. I wasn't thinking when I said the words—I know Ray thinks I'm ridiculous when I talk about my bad luck. I don't want Faith to think that. Even if she did believe me, she might worry about my bad luck rubbing off. And maybe she'd be right.

I want to change the subject, but Faith is waiting for an answer. I scramble through my thoughts and can't find an easy explanation. So I decide to give her the real one.

"I'm unlucky," I say. "Always have been. Always will be."

Faith pulls at her earlobe, like she does when she's thinking. "What does that mean exactly?"

I like how she doesn't tell me automatically that there's no such thing as unlucky. It's like she wants to hear more.

"It's something Ma told me," I say. "She said I was born under an unlucky star."

Faith raises her eyebrows. "So bad things happen to you? All the time?"

I nod. "Ever since I was little, things refuse to go my way. Ma explained that some people are born like that."

She watches me carefully. "What happened to your ma?"

I push at the wire, but it won't bend the way I want it to.

"She left," I say flatly. "When I was four."

Faith's eyes go round. "Bad luck," she whispers.

"The worst," I answer.

The silence stretches between us like bubble gum. I don't know what Faith's thinking right now, but I know what's on my mind.

Ma left because of me.

The thought feels like glancing at the sun. I know it's always there, but when I accidentally look at it directly, it hurts. I try my best to shove that thought away—to push it into the dark corners where it belongs. But no matter how much I try, the thought pops up like a stubborn balloon.

Faith is silent, pushing at the wire. It won't go the way she wants it to. She sighs in frustration, squeezing the metal. Then she clears her throat.

"You know how I said I'm staying at Aunt Louise's for a while?"

I nod, thinking back to the town meeting at Lulu's.

Faith takes a deep breath and then continues. "My mom has breast cancer. She's been at the hospital in Newford a lot, and my dad's been with her. They didn't want me at home alone."

Her words come out in a rush, like she had to hurry to get them out so she wouldn't use up all her air.

"My mom has four sisters," she continues. "The only one to get cancer. Bad luck, right?"

I nod, not knowing what to say. Newford is almost three hours from Oak Branch. Faith must be missing both of her parents so much.

Faith's voice shakes. "None of her sisters has it—just her. So maybe she was born under an unlucky star, like you."

I have to do something. *Anything.* I pat her arm. "I'm sorry."

She smooths the front of her shirt and straightens up. "Anyway. I hate talking about it. Let's work on the handle."

As we curve the chicken wire into a handle shape, my thoughts go a hundred miles an hour.

I hope Faith is wrong about her mom. I hope this is a spot of bad luck, not a downhill slide into unhappiness.

Bad luck is everywhere. First Gloria and now Faith. This whole time, I never imagined anyone else having bad luck like me. I should feel happy that I'm not alone anymore. But as I listen to Faith talk, I feel the weight of it like a boulder.

CHAPTER 20

Looking up at Gloria's house, Ray lets out a low whistle.

"This place needs a whole lot of work," he says.

"It's not so bad," I say. But when I look at it through Ray's eyes, I see the rotting wood trim, the peeling paint, the overgrown flower beds, and I know he's right.

Ray reaches out to the dangling shutter—the one I knocked loose that first day I checked on Gloria. The moment he touches it, it falls right off the house with a clatter.

He steps back. "Yikes. In a strong wind, this house would blow right over."

"Hush," I say firmly under my breath. "She'll hear you."

Otto's at the screen door, wagging his tail like a maniac.

"Hi, Otto! Good boy!" I tell him, which makes his tail wag even harder.

"Come on in, or you'll be arrested for loitering," Gloria shouts.

Ray's mouth drops open.

I shake my head and hold the door open, giving Otto ear scratches. "She's joking, Ray. Come on in."

His eyes widen but he follows me. I watch to see how Otto reacts, but he's in a friendly mood. He even wags his tail. No teeth, no barking. Ray, on the other hand, looks nervous. He holds his arms stiffly by his sides.

"Whoa," says Ray. "This is one unusual-looking dog."

"Distinct, you mean. He's one of a kind." I grin. "You should pet him."

Ray shifts uncomfortably. He's not used to being around dogs, either. But he lowers his hand toward Otto and begins patting him gently. Otto soaks up the attention, letting his tongue loll out of his mouth. Ray smiles and seems to relax a little.

"See, Otto?" I say. "Now you have a new friend."

Ray flashes a smile.

"Well!" Gloria says with a scowl. "Aren't you going to introduce me?" She reminds me of a queen, sitting in her armchair like that.

Ray gulps. He shoots me a look, not so relaxed anymore.

I shrug. I'm used to Gloria now. "This is my brother. Ray, this is Gloria Crumb."

"Hi," Ray says. I've already warned him not to try any of that *ma'am* business.

He turns to me, wrinkling his nose. "What's that smell?"

Otto sits between us, looking back and forth at us. He doesn't realize he's been insulted.

I frown, leaning over to scratch his ears. "Aw, come on, Ray. You'll hurt his feelings."

Ray shakes his head. "No—something else. Something *burning*."

I sniff deeply, and I can smell it, too. Together we head for the kitchen. The stove has been left on. A pot on top has boiled dry. Ray switches off the heat.

I slide open a window. "Yuck. It smells terrible."

"Told you," says Ray. He looks closer at the pan. "I think this pan is finished."

The outside of the pan is discolored, and the inside has a chalky black residue.

I head back to the front room. "Gloria, were you making tea?"

She looks surprised, then confused. It's like her thoughts are trying to connect back to what she did, but she can't quite get there.

"A pan boiled down to nothing," I say.

"Oh no," she says quietly.

"Ray turned it off," I tell her. "But I think the pan is ruined."

"I don't care about the pan," she says. "But promise me you won't tell Albert."

I look at her sideways. "I'm not sure, Gloria. That phone call was one thing, but this seems like it might be different."

"I get confused sometimes," she says. "It's like my brain is rusty. But it's only a little bit. It's because my arm's broken and I sit here bored all day. It's like my gears have seized up."

When I hear this, my stomach ties itself right in a knot. She thinks her brain is rusty, since she fell—and she fell because of *me*.

I fix her blanket, which has fallen on the floor. Then I return to the kitchen.

"We should call Dad," Ray says immediately.

I shake my head. "If Albert finds out about this, Gloria will have to go to a home."

Ray frowns. "Leaving the stove on is a big deal. It's electric, so at least there isn't a flame. But it still burned that pan—it's dangerous."

"She won't leave Otto," I say. "You can't do that to them."

Ray's lips press together in a line. I can tell he still wants to tell Dad. I have to stop him. If Gloria is sent away from Otto, I won't be able to bear it. It will be all my fault.

"Swear you won't tell anyone," I say. "Please, Ray."

Ray lets out a deep breath. "Annie, this is a *really* bad idea. She could get hurt."

I have to convince him. I can't let my bad luck rub off on her. It wouldn't be fair. Not to her. Not to Otto, either.

"I have an idea," I say. "We can compromise."

He looks at me skeptically.

I take a deep breath. "I think she's just confused because of her fall. She mixes up her words sometimes. Says her brain is rusty."

Ray shakes his head. "This sounds bad."

"If she goes somewhere Otto can't follow, I don't know what she'd do," I tell him.

Ray pauses. I know my brother. Underneath it all, he has a soft heart.

"What's the compromise?" he asks.

"If she isn't doing better by the time summer ends, I'll let Albert know," I say. "Okay?"

He frowns. "I don't know, Annie. What if she gets hurt?"

"Leaving Otto behind will hurt her the most," I say. "She's too old for a broken heart."

Ray is still for a long time. I know Ray thinks I'm being obstinate, but there's no way I can let this happen to Gloria and Otto.

"I think I can move the stove out enough to unplug it," he says finally. "You have to tell her, though."

I wait, holding my breath. He hasn't said anything about telling Dad.

Ray chews his lip. "If one other thing happens, even if it's small . . ."

I'm already nodding. "Even if it's itty-bitty. Even if it's *teensy*—"

He interrupts me. "You have to promise that you'll tell Albert. And Dad."

I breathe a sigh of relief. "You won't regret it—"

Ray narrows his eyes. "Not so fast, Annie. You have to promise or the deal is off. *Promise*. Swear it."

"Deal," I say breathlessly. "I promise. I swear."

Finally, he nods. Just once.

Something fierce comes over me. I grab Ray in a hug and squeeze him as tight as I can. "Thank you, Ray!"

He squirms away. "Okay, okay. That's enough of that."

His nose is wrinkled, but I see the corners of his mouth quirk up.

Ray heads outside with his toolbox and sets to work. I sit on the floor in the living room, sorting through boxes. I gaze at the room, feeling proud. Things are starting to look good in here, thanks to the fact that I've cleared out so many boxes.

Gloria says she understands about the stove being turned off. She even seems a little relieved. Together we watch her favorite game show, *Wheel of Fortune*. Gloria calls out the answers when she knows them. She gets a lot of them right, too.

The boxes are never labeled, so I never know what I'm going to see when I open the flaps. Sometimes it's old

Christmas ornaments wrapped in tissue paper. Another time it's office supplies—enough paper clips to last a lifetime.

I pull off the tape and peek at the next box, and right on top, there's a feather boa—it's purple. I pull it out of the box. Underneath are a silver crown and a pair of rainbow-striped knee socks.

I hold them up. "What's all this stuff?"

A slow smile spreads over Gloria's face. "That's from my roller-disco days."

I wrinkle my forehead. I understand the words but not the meaning. "Roller disco?"

She reaches out with her good arm. "Let me see."

I carry the items to her, shedding a trail of feathers behind me. Otto sniffs at one suspiciously.

"When I came back to take care of Mother, I used to go out to that roller rink on the edge of town. It was called . . ." Gloria closes her eyes in concentration. She opens them again, shaking her head. "Well, I'll remember it later. They were open every day. Tuesdays we could skate half-price. But Friday and Saturday nights were roller disco."

"What is that?"

Gloria's face softens, remembering. "There was music and lights. And we'd dance until it shut down. One night they named me queen—Queen of the Roller Disco."

She has a faraway look in her eye as she turns over the crown in her hand. "Thingamajig," she says in almost a whisper.

She's forgotten the word. "*Crown*. Or maybe *tiara*."

She glares at me. "I'm talking about the name of the rink! It was called Thingamajig."

"Oh. Sorry."

"The music was the best. So much fun. With a beat you could groove to." She starts humming and singing something that sounds like "boogie oogie oogie."

I pinch my arm so I don't laugh. Gloria Crumb grooving on roller skates. The world is full of surprises.

I turn back to the box, flipping through old photos. They're all at the roller-skating rink. The photographs are faded, but the smiles are bright. Gloria with a group of friends, looking at something off camera. Then another, wearing a sparkly jumpsuit. Then there's one of her by herself, in the center of a circle, everyone watching. She has white skates with pink wheels and pom-poms on the laces. Gloria is leaping into the air, a blur—but even so, I can see that she's smiling wider than I've ever seen her do in person.

"You were really good!" I try to keep the surprise out of my voice, but I can't hide it. These pictures show a Gloria Crumb I never could have imagined. I know the Gloria Crumb who's crabby all the time—who leaves a pot on the stove and almost burns down her house. But these pictures show Gloria Crumb, always laughing. Gloria Crumb, the roller-disco queen.

I hold up the photos. "Do you want to see these?"

But Gloria shakes her head. "Better to forget. What good will those memories do me now?"

"But, Gloria," I say. "You look so happy."

She scowls. "I don't want to talk about it. You've tired me out, girl. I need to take a rest."

She hobbles down the hall to her bedroom door and shuts it firmly.

I look at Otto and shrug. I can still hear Ray whistling outside.

Otto comes over and lies next to me, tail thumping in slow motion. His eyes droop, and he seems like he needs a rest, too.

I rub behind his ears, where the fur grows thick and soft. The open screen door lets in the smell of pine trees and the growl of a distant lawn mower. Ray is on the front porch, nailing and hammering—and, of course, whistling while he works. Each time Ray hits a high note, Otto's ears twitch and he opens his eyes again.

"He's not so bad," I whisper. "Once you get to know him."

I know he doesn't understand my words, but he relaxes anyway—as if he was waiting for me to say them. He lets out a deep sigh and falls asleep.

CHAPTER
21

When we finish at Gloria's, Ray says he's going to Tyler's house, which obviously I have no interest in.

I already know Faith is in Newford visiting her mom today. No one's at the park. I wander over the lake bridge and end up at Logan & Son. At least I can get some popcorn from the machine.

The store is empty, which is a bad sign. Sundays can be busy, even though we're open for only a few hours. But at least Dad brightens when he sees me.

Then I see why and my heart sinks.

"Cleaning day," he says cheerfully.

I groan. A store cleaning day is *way* more involved than mopping and dusting. For a cleaning day, we attack the store one section at a time. First, we take each item off the shelves and clean it. Then we scrub the shelves.

Finally, we put everything back. It's incredibly boring. I'd rather hold a hundred ladders.

"Come on, Annie," Dad says. "It's not so bad. I'll pay you in popcorn."

"Our popcorn is *free*," I grumble.

Instead of answering, he hands me spray cleaner and a rag. I sigh and start scrubbing shelves.

The truth is, once I get started, it isn't so bad. In a hardware store, the shelves do get dusty. There's something satisfying about seeing everything become organized and sparkling clean.

Dad seems to be in a good mood. Like Ray, he whistles while he works.

"How was your time at Gloria's?" he asks.

I shrug. "I thought it was okay. Maybe even good. We were looking at old pictures. Then she got upset all of a sudden."

Dad glances at me. "Dredging up those old memories might be hard on her."

Figures that he would think that. He's the one who'll never talk about Ma.

"I don't know about that," I say. "I think it's good to remember things."

"I'm glad you're helping her," Dad says quietly.

I pick at some gunk with my fingernail. All day I've been thinking of the roller-skating version of Gloria.

"She was a roller-disco queen," I say. "Did you know that?"

Dad shakes his head, smiling. "I had no idea."

"She's had this whole big life," I say. "You'd never know it now, the way she sits in her chair in her house all day long. She doesn't seem like someone who was a roller-disco queen, a babysitter, a grumpy old lady, a flight attendant."

Dad puts clean boxes back on the shelf.

"She took care of all her brothers and sisters," I continue. "She rode a mule at the Grand Canyon. She's been a hundred versions of herself. Which one is the real Gloria?"

"Maybe she's all those things together," says Dad absentmindedly. Then he looks at what I'm doing. "Don't spray so much cleaner."

I ignore him. Spraying the cleaner is the best part of a cleaning day.

"So, Dad—do we have a box like that with pictures of Ma?" I blurt it out. Someday I'll learn to ease into these kinds of questions.

Dad stiffens. "She didn't like pictures—you've seen all we have. Why do you ask?"

"I guess I was thinking it might give us a clue about where she went," I say. "If we knew there was a specific adventure she wanted to have."

And this is what I think but don't say: *If I knew more about her, maybe we could find her. Maybe we could know when she's coming back.*

"She wanted a different life," Dad says. "One I couldn't give her."

"But why—"

Dad shakes his head. "Sometimes questions don't have answers."

He sets down his cloth and moves on to the next section. He's only a few feet from me but it feels like he's a mile away.

To him, the subject is closed. To me, it feels unfinished. But I don't know how to say the question written in my heart.

Was I the reason she left?

CHAPTER 22

Otto is slowly becoming a different dog.

Not literally. He still has the same crooked teeth, the same strange look about him. But he's calmer. He doesn't bark as much. And the more I spend time with him in the backyard, the happier he seems.

We haven't quite conquered the front yard yet. Earlier this week, I put a leash on him. I figured that was the first step to eventually taking a walk outside. But he did not appreciate it. He plopped down in the doorway and eyed me suspiciously.

"Otto," I told him. "Have a little faith in me, would you?"

He didn't budge, of course. But since then, I've been putting the leash on him each day to try to help him get used to it. He's wearing it now, inside, even though he's pouting about it.

After I say hello to Gloria, I go to the kitchen to make her a new batch of tea. Now that her stove is switched off, I use the microwave to heat the water. I do it just like she tells me and am careful not to squeeze the tea bags. I pour her a glass over ice and take it to her in the living room.

She sips it, shuddering. "Too sweet. If my teeth haven't fallen out by the end of summer, it will be a miracle."

I shake my head. But she drinks it anyway, taking small bites from the cookies I put on a plate for her.

She pats her mouth with a napkin. "These cookies are decent. Did you make them?"

"They're from Lulu's," I say. I was surprised this morning when I saw Dad carrying the pink box. He said something about helping Faith's aunt Louise with a project—I guess he decided to overlook his usual policy on healthy eating.

Gloria takes a bite of a citrus crisp, then another. For someone so picky about sugar in tea, she doesn't seem to mind these sugary cookies. Typical Gloria.

Otto stands up and walks over to her, trying to sniff the food.

Gloria nibbles her cookie. "These aren't for you."

Otto pushes his nose against her.

"Sakes alive!" Gloria says, shooing him away. "You've had him on this leash long enough; maybe you should try taking him out."

I pick up the end of the leash and pull Otto away. It takes some effort, but eventually we reach the doorway. I step onto the porch, but he won't come outside. He's frozen with either fear or stubbornness—I can't tell which.

"Come on, Otto!" I say.

He plants his rear on the threshold.

"Otto," I say in my most encouraging voice. "Let's go!"

It doesn't do any good. The more I talk to him, the more he seems glued to the floor. Eventually he lies down, stretching his paws and yawning in a way that lets me know he is thoroughly unimpressed.

I sigh. Maybe this is it. Maybe this is the best he can do.

I sit on the porch next to him, still holding the leash even though I know he's not going anywhere.

"I want to give you a more interesting life, Otto. Remember that squirrel in the backyard? There are lots of interesting things to look at if we go for a walk. We could go to the park. Or if that's too far, we could go to the corner. See the sweet gum tree? In the fall, they drop sticker balls that hurt your feet like anything if you step on them barefoot. But we know how to watch where we step, right, Otto?"

I set down the leash. He doesn't need one when he's too afraid to place a single paw on the porch.

"The wide world is scary sometimes," I tell him. "But I promise you'll be okay."

I reach over and scratch him behind the ears. He rewards me with a thump of his tail. I rub his chest, where his fur swirls like a whirlpool.

Sometimes when I pet Otto, I think about how he needs people to make sure he's safe. Maybe that's the point of having a pet. There's something special about being in charge of a life like that.

I stand up. Otto watches me with his crooked eyes. Slowly I take four steps backward, looking at him the whole time. I reach out my hands.

"Otto," I whisper. "*Come.*"

He stands up and shakes himself. I hold my breath.

Then he lies down again.

I sigh.

He grins and lets that tongue roll out, like he's very proud of himself.

I lower myself to the porch next to him. He nudges me with his nose, and I reach over to give him ear scratches.

"There's more to the world than what's in your backyard, Otto," I whisper. "Someday, I hope you'll let me show you."

CHAPTER 23

It's Friday, and the festival is two weeks away—which means people are working on their floats all kinds of hours. Except for Dad and Ray.

The float for Lulu's is turning out great. Faith and I have been building up the papier-mâché layers on the coffee cup nicely. As soon as they're dry, we'll be able to start painting.

I walk around to see if anyone needs help with their floats. It's nice to see the progress and talk with people about how things are coming. Everyone is so excited, talking about the festival and how this is finally going to put Oak Branch on the map.

People trickle out as the afternoon warms up, but I keep on working. I'm painting some of the food for JoJo and The Earl's float and barely register the fact that time is passing. But as the sun gets low in the sky, the light in the barn turns golden. It's time for Friday night dinner with Dad and Ray.

I close the barn door behind me and walk through downtown. Shops are closing, but there are quite a few people out tonight. We may not get lots of tourists, but I like seeing the familiar faces of people I know as I walk by.

I reach Logan & Son as Ray is flipping the Open sign to Closed. He opens the door for me.

"Dad's counting out the register," he says. "Do you want to mop the floors or take out the trash?"

I make a face. If I'd been a little later, I could have missed the end-of-day chores.

"Trash, I guess."

Ray gets out the mop, and soon the smell of fake pine trees—nowhere near as good as real ones—fills the store. I go behind the register and grab the bin under the counter. Dad counts the money in tidy piles. I can't help noticing that the stacks seem smaller than they should be.

When I come back from the big garbage can in the alley, I wash my hands and return to the register. Dad twists a rubber band around the bills and puts them in the bank envelope. The worry lines in his forehead are deep.

"Hey, Dad. Tough day?"

He looks startled. "Oh, a bit, I guess."

I want to ask him more, but he turns away to straighten the back counter. He is quick and efficient as he files receipts, sorts papers, and adds to his to-do list. Practical and predictable. I wander through the aisles, even though there's nothing new to see.

After Ray puts away the mop, he comes over to me.

"Where's Dad?" he asks.

I look around in time to see Dad coming out of the back washroom. He's holding a toothbrush.

He's careful about brushing and flossing of course, but this seems a bit over-the-top.

"Dad?" I ask. "Did you just *brush your teeth*? On the way to dinner?"

Dad gets a funny look on his face. I look at Ray, who shrugs.

"Had something with garlic for lunch," Dad says quickly. "I think it upset my system a bit."

I wrinkle my nose. "Ew, Dad."

Outside, the sky is turning orange. We walk down the block to JoJo & The Earl's. After hugs from JoJo and procuring a handful of root beer candy, Ray and I head for our regular table, split down the middle as always.

I slide onto the yellow side and Ray sits on red, but Dad is standing near a six-seater table on the red side.

"We could try this one for a change," he says.

Ray and I exchange glances.

"No way," I say. "I'm not sitting on the red side."

"This is tradition," Ray says. "Besides, we don't need a big table."

Dad hesitates for a moment, but then he nods. He slides in next to Ray on the red side.

Ray flips open his menu. "I'm starving—I think I'm going to order extra food. Green beans, corn, and ribs, too—"

Dad closes his menu quickly and hops to his feet. "Well, hey," he calls out.

I look toward the door, where Faith is standing with her aunt Louise.

"Hi," I say, waving. Faith waves back.

That's a coincidence. I've never seen Faith and Louise here on Friday nights. They come over to say hi.

"Hi," Dad says. "Scoot over, Annie."

I almost choke on my root beer candy. Wait a minute—what's happening here? We've never had anyone join us for Friday night dinner.

But it's too late. Faith is sitting next to me, and Dad offers Louise his spot. He grabs a chair from a different table and sits on the end.

I shoot a look at Ray—"Did you know about this?" But he shakes his head and goes back to his menu.

I glance at Faith, but she's laughing at Dad's joke. *Dad.* Making a joke.

Now Dad and Louise are chatting about the festival and business in Oak Branch. Dad is grinning like I've never seen him do before. A lump forms in my throat and spreads to the bottom of my stomach. This isn't a coincidence. This was planned. And Dad didn't even ask us.

Faith bumps my elbow. She's looking my way, wanting me to laugh at whatever Dad said. But I can't talk when I can't even think. I stare at my menu like it's the most fascinating thing on Earth.

I don't even recognize this Dad, who's folding his paper napkin into a crane. I didn't even know he could do that. It seems like something I should have known.

"Annie," Louise says. "I love all the work you've done on our float. Faith told me you have such creative ideas."

I try to force a smile, but I can tell it comes out weird. My words stick in my throat. Ray, for his part, seems to have recovered from the shock. He launches into a story about his maker space idea *again*.

I sink low in my seat. How can I talk when I can't even think? Balloons of questions crowd my mind. How long has this been going on? Are Dad and Louise *dating*?

I can see the writing on the wall. Dad and Louise are on their way to falling in love, if they haven't already. Officially ending the story of Dad and Ma. Officially giving up hope that she's ever coming back.

Well, I'm not ready to give up on that.

PART FOUR

Balloons

From the Collected Drawings of Annie P. Logan

Dimensions: 9" × 12"

CHAPTER
24

Dad never explained why Faith and her aunt Louise joined us, and I haven't wanted to ask. I keep my distance. Anyhow, I'm busy with Gloria, Otto, and the floats.

On Sunday, after church and pancakes, I stop to change my clothes before heading to Gloria's. Life is much better when wearing comfortable clothes. I pick shorts, a T-shirt, and my favorite green sweatshirt, which is the exact color of a meadow in May.

"I'll come by later to help with those projects," Ray says.

So later, at Gloria's, I'm not surprised to see him coming up the walk. I am surprised, though, when I see that he isn't alone. Walking alongside him, right up the path, are his basketball friends: Javier, Grant, and *Tyler*. They're carrying cans of paint, rollers, masking tape, and a canvas drop cloth.

Otto is beside me and has the good sense to start barking.

Grant nods at me, and Javier says, "Hey, Annie." But Tyler is quiet, which is very unlike him. He looks at the front door, then down the driveway across the street to the park. I can tell he's putting the pieces together—he knows this is the doorbell I was supposed to ring that day.

I burst out the screen door. "What are *they* doing here?"

Ray frowns, puzzled. "I told them there were lots of projects. They said they could help."

I cross my arms and look at them. "Y'all know you can't get community service hours by helping here, right? You should go to the barn instead. They need help with the floats."

Javier raises his eyebrows. Grant widens his eyes. Tyler is still looking back and forth between the house and the park.

Ray glares at me. "That's rude, Annie. I can't do this on my own."

"I'll help," I say.

Ray rolls his eyes. "I've seen the way you hold ladders. No thanks."

I step back. Ray and I may not always get along, but he's usually not so direct about it.

I sigh. "I have to ask Gloria. It's her house, you know."

Not waiting for a response, I step inside. The screen door slams shut behind me. Otto is still barking at the boys.

Gloria frowns. "What's got him so upset?"

I knew she wouldn't want them here.

"There's a bunch of boys outside—my brother and his friends," I tell her. "Ray thought they would do some work on your house, but I know you don't like visitors. I'll tell them to go."

I head for the door, but Gloria lifts up her good hand. "They're here to help?"

"Yes," I say slowly.

Gloria sits up a little straighter. "How *lovely*. I'd like to meet them."

I'm not sure what I was expecting, but this reaction was not it. I didn't think Gloria ever used a word like "lovely."

I march back to the screen door. Otto hasn't budged and is still barking. At least *he's* on my side.

"Hush, Otto," I tell him, even though I wouldn't mind if he chased them away. I wait until he sits before I open the screen door.

"She wants to meet you," I say.

The boys file in and stand near the wall, like a police lineup. Grant squirms like he's about to flee.

"Hi," Ray says. "Didn't mean to trouble you."

Gloria pats her hair. "Annie says you're here to help. Such gentlemen!"

Her voice is suddenly a stack of pancakes with extra-sticky syrup on top. Of all the Glorias I've known, I've never seen sweet Gloria. I didn't even know that one existed. I guess she was saving it for perfect Ray and his perfect friends.

I fold my arms tight and look levelly at Gloria.

"They're just boys," I say.

Gloria fully ignores me and continues beaming at them. I feel a flash of irritation. I've been here every single day and never once has she smiled at *me* like that.

Her eyes sparkle. "What a special treat. Your families must be so proud of their young men."

Ugh. This is so typical. When girls do something nice, it's an expectation. When boys do something nice, it's a *celebration.*

Tyler does a little half wave. "I'm Tyler Barnes, the mayor's son."

I roll my eyes. Leave it to Tyler to work that into the conversation. At least Javier and Grant have the decency to mumble their names awkwardly.

Ray looks at me, as if I'm going to help. But I shake my head. This was his idea—*he* can figure it out.

Tyler cuts his eyes at me for a second, then looks back at Gloria. "Can I ask, ma'am, how you hurt your arm?"

I glare at Tyler.

The good news is, his nosiness about her arm seems to have broken the spell Gloria was under. Her eyes narrow in a frown.

"That's a little personal, young man. Off to work with all of you!" Her tone is crisp and businesslike, and they listen to her, heading into the backyard. After a moment I can hear them dragging things around back there.

Gloria pulls at a loose thread on her blanket. "They remind me of Albert when he was that age. All elbows and knees—they grow so fast. I could hardly keep the kitchen stocked for the times he'd come over."

I nod. "Dad always says that Ray eats his weight in groceries and then some."

"Such a very long time ago," she says, almost to herself. Then she glances at me again, like she's suddenly remembered that I exist. "See if we have some snacks for them, in case they're hungry later. Albert always liked those crackers with the cheese."

I want to point out that I'm *also* growing. She's never offered me anything to eat. These are just boys, wild boys like her brothers who she likes to complain about. I want to tell her that, but something in her expression stops me. She's looking into the distance, lost in her memories. So I don't say a word.

In the kitchen, I find the crackers and pour some tea for Gloria. But when I return, she's fallen asleep in her armchair.

Her blanket has slid onto the floor, and Otto is sprawled on top of it.

"Otto," I say softly. "Off the blanket."

He thumps his tail hopefully.

"This isn't for you," I tell him. "I don't want her to get a chill."

I grab the edge of the blanket and somehow get it out from under him. Then I place it on her lap.

Otto lets out a high-pitched cry.

I frown, looking around. He isn't hungry and he doesn't want to go out. Then it dawns on me.

"You want a blanket?"

His tail swings wildly.

I sigh. "She needs it. I don't have another one."

But I can't say no to his hopeful face. I untie my green sweatshirt from around my waist and place it on the floor.

"That's my favorite sweatshirt, so you better be nice to it," I tell him.

He lies down on it happily and rolls on his back. I can't help but smile. He is a dog with good taste in sweatshirts.

I turn back to Gloria. She looks different now, sleeping. If she'd let me, I'd draw her like this. It reminds me of the time I noticed her with Otto—how she seemed softer somehow.

"I'm sorry," I tell her in a whisper. "I'm sorry I came up to your driveway that day. I'm sorry I was going to ring your doorbell. And I'm sorry that I let everyone think I'm helping you because I'm a good person, because I'm not. I'm sorry my bad luck rubbed off on you."

She snores lightly.

I walk quietly so I don't wake her up. Carefully, I close the door behind me. I smile, thinking of them like that— Gloria snoozing while Otto snuggles my favorite sweatshirt. Even though I know she didn't hear my apology, at least I said it. That should count for something.

CHAPTER
25

When Ray and his friends finish, I tell them to come out the side gate so we don't disturb Gloria and Otto. Together we walk through downtown. The boys carry all the painting supplies. They don't ask for help and I don't offer. I dawdle a few steps behind, hoping to avoid any questions. Tyler glances at me a couple of times, but he doesn't say a peep about the day I rang Gloria's doorbell.

Outside Dad's store, Ray stops. "We can take it from here. Thanks for helping."

They place the painting gear on the sidewalk and say, "See you later." Once they walk away, Ray turns to me, squinting.

"Don't you want to say anything?" he asks.

"To them? Not really," I say.

Ray raises his eyebrows. "Typical."

I frown. "What's your problem?"

Ray kicks at some pebbles on the sidewalk and watches them scatter. "Never mind." He picks up a canvas drop cloth and starts folding it.

I watch. For the record, folding a drop cloth is *ridiculous*. There's no reason to arrange something neatly when its whole purpose in life is to catch messy paint splatters. He's just doing it to make a point about how perfect he is.

The more he folds, the madder I get. It's like each crisp edge and sharp corner is stabbing me. Good old perfect Ray. It's not enough for him to help when I ask him to; he has to show up when I *don't* ask him to. He has to bring an army of friends, including Tyler—who will likely blab to someone about Ding-Dong Ditch, and then I will land in a heap of trouble.

I cross my arms tightly across my chest. "You should have told me you were bringing your friends today, not just shown up with them like that."

Ray looks up from his drop cloth, frowning. "I don't get it. You *asked* for help."

"I don't know why you hang out with Tyler," I go on. "He's always asking fake questions and being fakey-fake nice to people. *I'm the mayor's son.* He's so smarmy."

Ray's face flushes. "He *is* the mayor's son. And he's not smarmy—it's called being nice. You could stand to be a little nicer yourself."

Now I'm steaming. "What is that supposed to mean?"

Ray shakes his head. "They helped for *free*. They didn't even get service hours for school. And you couldn't even say hi, which was completely awkward and embarrassing."

There's a roaring in my ears, like I'm suddenly underwater. Ray thinks I'm awkward and embarrassing. I *embarrass* him by my awkward existence. I know I'm a stubborn person. I know I don't have friends at school. But I never thought my own brother felt this way. And even if he did, I never thought he'd ever say it to my face.

"You're so nasty all the time," Ray continues. "Do you think no one noticed that at Friday dinner you barely said a word to Faith or Louise? Faith is your friend and still you treat her that way."

I try to swallow, but it's like something is stuck in my throat. I would never be mean to *Faith* of all people.

"I was just trying to understand what was going on with Dad and Louise. Maybe if I didn't get left out all the time, I wouldn't have been so surprised," I say.

Ray glares at me. "Seriously, you are the biggest baby I know."

"Well, at least one of us isn't acting like a mini grown-up," I say. "Trying to be such a big shot, acting like you know how to expand the hardware store—"

Ray hurls the drop cloth to the ground, where it lands in a heap. "The store that's losing money every month. The store that's hanging on by a tiny thread because Dad can't see that he needs to try something new. I'm so tired of being in this family that's stuck doing things the way they've always been done."

My breath catches; my mind whirls with new information. I know Dad's been worried and preoccupied, but I didn't think the store was losing money. That can't be true, can it?

"Well, I'm tired of being stuck in this family that eats oatmeal every day," I say. "I wish Ma would come home. I miss spaghetti dinners in the bathtub. I miss frozen-waffle picnics in the park. I miss everything we had. And I want it back."

Ray rolls his eyes. "Ma is never coming back, Annie. I can't believe you think she'll show up and want to be our mom again. No more spaghetti, no more waffles. No more dog bites because she wasn't even watching us."

The lump in my throat is expanding. I can barely breathe, let alone talk. "How dare you say that! You are a lot of things, Raymond K. Logan, but I never knew you were so *disloyal*."

Ray growls in frustration, running both hands through his hair like he wants to rip it out. "Because it's *true*. She left. She's never coming back."

I don't want to hear it. I shake my head like it will push his words away.

"You don't understand because you have Dad," I tell him. "But she left me all alone."

Ray shakes his head tightly. "You aren't alone. You have Dad and me. You have JoJo and The Earl and Faith and all kinds of people in this town."

Hot, prickly tears pop into my eyes. "Maybe that's true for you, but it isn't for me. Everyone gets along with perfect Ray. You have it easy."

Ray's face flickers with emotion. The muscle in his jaw tenses. His hand turns into a fist. I automatically step aside. But instead of hitting me, he punches the wall.

"Augh!" Ray shouts, swinging his hand back and forth like it's on fire.

I gasp, covering my mouth in shock. "What in the world? Did you break your hand?"

His eyes are bright and wet. "It's *not* easy for me!"

My mouth hangs open. I'm stunned. "I—What?"

"She . . . left . . . me . . . too," he says in a halting voice. Each word is sharp and solid, with fully formed edges.

My mind is blank. I hear his words but can't sort their meaning.

He takes a deep breath and lets it out in a shudder.

"It happened to me, too," he says. "Ma left me, too. You act like it only happened to you, but it didn't. She left all of us."

I gulp. "Ray, I didn't—"

"Yes, you did," he says. "You always do. You are so selfish. You are the most selfish person I've ever met."

Before I can speak, he turns and walks away.

I want to yell. I want to make him turn around. The words burn in my throat, but I can't make myself talk. Instead, I just watch him go.

CHAPTER
26

Ray isn't supposed to get mad. He and Dad are supposed to be alike. Practical. Predictable. Always holding it together.

But patient, steady, *perfect* Ray has stormed off, and I'm standing on the sidewalk with only a drop cloth for company.

I need to get away. I turn in the opposite direction from the way Ray is heading. I don't know where I'm going, but my feet make a plan for me. I end up at the barn. When I push the heavy door open, the sharp-sweet sawdust smell hits me and smooths a bit of my jagged edges.

I'm the only one there, and I'm glad. I switch the radio on and spin the dial until I hear the zippy fiddles of the bluegrass station. Then I turn and survey the barn.

The floats are so familiar, it feels like seeing friends. I walk by them one by one—JoJo & The Earl's table piled high with a barbecue feast, the bookshelves at Oak Branch Books dotted with rosy maple moths, the H. Diggity hot dog loaded with toppings. The floats are full of personality, just like all the shops and restaurants in our town. The only exception is the one in the corner. The float Dad and Ray started but never finished. The one that says our family is broken, busted, and missing a piece. The float that says our family can't work together.

I go closer to take a better look. The base is sturdy, probably the strongest in the barn. But that's all it is—a base.

I'm so frustrated, I give it a good kick.

"Ow!"

Stars dance in my vision. I feel dizzy, so I ease myself into a sit. While I rub my foot, I look at the wood planks and recognize the design from Ray's diagrams.

Ray may be perfect, but this float sure isn't. Dad may be practical and predictable, but a float without something beautiful is worse than pointless—it's a waste. A solid structure is important, but it needs something more to make it shine.

I may be selfish, but I know art. I know how to make a parade float come alive.

I'm tired of everything unsaid in my family. I head to the metal lockers where supplies are kept. I get chicken wire, zip ties, and bundles of newspapers. And then I get to work.

CHAPTER 27

I build and cut and glue until my fingers are numb and my eyes are crossed from strain. My mouth is scratchy, and I can't remember the last time I ate or drank. There's a chill in the air, which makes me wish I still had the green sweatshirt I left under a napping Otto.

But in front of me, I see *something*—where before, there was nothing. To me, that's the exact definition of making art.

People come and go in the barn, but I'm focused on my project. I don't look up—that is, not until I hear someone calling my name.

"Annie," JoJo says. "Sit down and have something to eat."

In one hand, she holds a plate stacked high with all my favorites—Eastern-style barbecue, boiled potatoes, and corn sticks. In the other, she holds an extra-tall glass of lemonade.

As soon as I notice the food, my stomach lets out a rumble. I haven't eaten since this morning, but I hadn't even realized I was hungry.

I look around, blinking. "What time is it anyway?"

"Almost nine," says JoJo.

I smack my forehead. "Dad's going to be mad—"

But she's shaking her head. "I was up here earlier and saw you working hard. Popped by the store to say I'd take you supper and make sure you get home safe. I told him not to wait up."

We find a pair of chairs, and I tuck in to my plate. It's delicious as always. Hot and spicy and sweet, and of course the very best part—made with love.

When I finish, I wipe my mouth. "Now what?"

"You tell me," she says. "Why don't you put me to work?"

My eyebrows pop up. "Really?"

She nods firmly. "You've helped with every float in here. Now I'm going to help you."

I should probably be polite and tell her no, but my glance falls on a pile of pink and yellow fabric. I hesitate. "If you're sure, I could use some help with my moths. They're a little skimpy."

She rubs her hands together, grinning. "Let me at them."

I show her the materials, and JoJo sets to fattening up my moths. She twists and turns the strips of pink and yellow material. Her hands are quick and agile, reminding me of the way she weaves the lattice tops for her cherry pies.

She holds one out to admire.

"That's better," she says, a note of satisfaction in her voice.

"Much better," I agree. "No one likes a skinny moth."

Her eyes twinkle, and she reaches for another. We settle into a rhythm. I cut the strips of material, and JoJo wraps the bodies. After that, I add the eyes and antennae. Even if no one will appreciate these details from a distance, I love making their funny faces. There's something magic about seeing their transformation from puny creatures into their fuzzy and fabulous selves.

My fingers fly as I try to match her pace. And as busy as my hands are, I guess my thoughts are, too—because suddenly my mind is crowded with thoughts. All the thoughts about Ray I've pushed away are suddenly right there in my head and I can't escape them. They run in an endless loop. Our fight. The way he said I embarrass him. How he yelled. The way he punched the wall.

I wish JoJo could fix it for us. We need someone to twist up our problems and tuck in all our edges.

When I look up, she's watching me. "Everything okay, sugar?"

I clear my throat. "I messed up. With Ray."

She twirls fabric around the moth abdomen, which is turning plumper by the second. "Whatever it is, I'm sure you two can work it out."

I set down my antennae. "Not sure about that, JoJo. He was real mad. I always knew we were different, but now I know we aren't one bit alike. We're complete opposites."

She's quiet for a long time. Finally, she fixes me with her blue gaze. Not fierce like Gloria's but soft like a pair of faded jeans.

"Did I ever tell you about Dale?" she asks.

I shake my head.

She sighs and sets down the moth. "My first husband."

"Oh," I say, surprised. I think I knew technically that she had one, but she never talks about him.

"We were terrible together," she says. "We'd fight like cats and dogs, yelling and screaming, always struggling to prove who was right."

It's all I can do to keep my mouth from dropping open. JoJo's voice is like the satin-ribbon border on a cozy blanket. Imagining her screaming is absolutely impossible.

I frown. "What happened?"

"He traveled with his work. Long trips," JoJo says. "And one day he'd been gone for a while, and I realized he was never coming back. Left me with our two little boys."

My brain jumps around like electricity. *JoJo got left, too.*

"I remember the day I filed the papers to end our marriage. I was sure I wouldn't fall in love again," she continues. "Too much trouble. Too much pain."

She sighs, shaking her head. "But then I met The Earl. He swooped in with that big personality of his. And made me feel like he'd always be there for me—for the boys, too, even though they were grown by then."

I smile, thinking of the story of their restaurant. Right down the middle, representing each of them equally.

"You and The Earl are the exact definition of 'happily ever after.' You never argue," I say.

Her eyes crinkle in a smile. "It's okay to disagree with someone you love. He and I do our share of it."

My jaw really does drop this time. "But y'all are the two biggest lovebirds I've ever seen."

She laughs. "Even people who like each other a whole lot—who *love* each other—have conflicts sometimes. But we always try to see the other's perspective. Sometimes that's what love is—putting aside the notion of being right and instead being just plain curious about the person you're talking to."

I never thought about it that way. But I'm not thinking about JoJo and The Earl. Instead, I'm thinking about my parents.

I look at her carefully, weighing my words. "Did Ma and Dad fight like cats and dogs, too?"

JoJo's eyes widen. I've never asked her about Ma before. But I never wanted answers as much as I do now.

"Not that I ever saw, honey," she says quietly.

Disappointment crawls into my chest. I cross my arms. She looks at me like she can tell I'm upset.

Her forehead creases in confusion. "Were you hoping that they did?"

"It's not that I *wanted* them to fight," I say. "But a reason would be nice—something that makes sense."

"Have you tried asking your dad?" she asks.

I bite my lip. "He doesn't believe that old memories should be dredged up."

She nods. We're quiet, for a while, like that.

"Do you want me to tell you about your ma?"

Her voice is so gentle, it makes tears pop into my eyes.

"More than anything in the world," I tell her, and I mean it sincerely.

"She liked to walk in the rain," JoJo says, remembering. "People worried because she'd take you and Ray with her, even if it was cold. But she was careful—bundling you in a baby carrier and Ray in his yellow slicker and frog boots."

My breath catches. The way she describes it is like a picture. "The kind of carrier where the baby rides in the front?"

JoJo smiles. "Exactly that kind."

I knew it! I rode in a baby carrier, just like Fabian. I can practically feel Ma kissing the top of my head. I don't have that empty-balloon feeling. For the first time in ages, I feel full and warm.

I also feel greedy for more of these little bits of Ma.

"What else?" I try to sound casual, but inside I'm memorizing every word.

JoJo looks into the distance, but I can see the warmth glowing in her eyes. "She liked my chess pie. You're supposed to let it cool, but she'd only eat it straight from the oven. I used to call her when I was baking one."

I look at JoJo sideways. "Didn't that bother her? I bet she burned her mouth."

JoJo shakes her head. "Other things bothered her, but never the pie."

I lean forward so far, I almost fall over. "What do you mean, *other things bothered her?*" This feels like the clue I've been waiting for—the thing that will help me understand.

JoJo shrugs. "She had bad days, where she couldn't get out of bed. Other times, she'd walk for miles, like she had a motor inside pushing her on."

"Is there anything else?" I ask. "It feels like I'm missing pieces to a jigsaw puzzle."

JoJo studies my face. "What is it you're looking for exactly, Annie? Let me know how to help."

Her words are soft, but they hit me hard. I thought it was obvious. *Ma.* I'm looking for *Ma.* I don't say the words, but I think them so loud, it's like my brain is shouting. I want something real about her, not a floating balloon that's just out of reach.

"I understand what you're saying about marriage—at least I think so. But what—" I start to say, but something catches in my throat. The words feel like spikeballs, and it hurts to keep them in.

"What made her leave me?" I pause, remembering Ray's words on the sidewalk outside the store. *Ma left me, too.*

I shake my head. "*Us.* Me and Ray."

The question felt strong on the inside, but the words squeak out in a whisper.

JoJo reaches for my hand, tracing my dog-bite scars. "She was miserable after this happened. She wouldn't leave the hospital even for a single minute."

I frown. She must not have been *too* worried, because she left as soon as I got better.

"Your dad was frantic with worry—about his little girl in the hospital, about his wife who couldn't stop crying," JoJo continues. "Such a tiny hand. Lucky it wasn't even more serious."

I pull my hand away. "Nothing lucky about it."

I look down at the moths. I feel like crushing them one by one.

JoJo studies my face for a moment. "Her thinking wasn't right, Annie, but it had nothing to do with how much she loved you. I think she honestly believed you and Ray would be better off without her."

We go back to our work. I can tell she thinks she's eased my mind. I don't have the heart to tell her she's churned everything up even more.

Balloons of questions swarm in my head. Hearing that Ma was worried about me should make me feel happier, but instead I spark with anger. Maybe I was lucky that the dog bite wasn't worse—that I don't have permanent damage. But then Ma left, which was the worst thing that could happen.

I remember Gloria's words. *Not luck. Just life.* But what about when your entire life is bad luck?

CHAPTER
28

The next morning, I'm exhausted. I wake up thinking of Faith. We haven't talked since the dinner at JoJo & The Earl's. I need to find her.

I get dressed and head downtown. I push the door open at Lulu's, and Faith is behind the counter, wearing an apron.

"Hi," I say. "Can I have a corn muffin?"

She shrugs and puts one in a bag. "That's all?"

I gulp. "Do you want to go somewhere and talk?"

She looks like she's thinking it over, but Louise appears out of nowhere, smiling. "You two go ahead. No charge on that, Annie."

Faith hangs her apron in the back and appears a minute later, holding a berry muffin for herself.

"Come on," she says, and I follow her.

I think we're going to the back patio, but instead she heads for an opening in the trees. Before I know it, we're down at the lake. There's a big boulder that's wedged on the shoreline, half in the water and half out of it.

Without a word, Faith kicks off her shoes and crawls onto the rock. I do the same, but she just looks into the distance, picking the raspberries out of the muffin and eating them one by one. I wonder if we're still friends or if I managed to mess that up, too.

The sweet corn taste sticks in my throat.

"Are you mad at me or something?" I ask.

"After the way you acted at dinner, I thought you were mad at me," she says coolly.

I take a deep breath. What I want to say is: "Faith, I'm having a really bad couple of days, so if you want to tell me something, just do it."

What really happens is this: I start crying. Big sobs squeeze through my body and push out of me like they have a mind of their own. It's like every bit of sadness from yesterday has chosen this moment to come squeezing through my body.

Faith's eyes widen. "Annie, are you okay?"

I swing my head back and forth. I'm not okay. I'm not.

She grabs my elbow. "Stick your feet in the water."

I look at her, confused. "My feet in the—Why?"

She shakes her head, exasperated. "Annie, you don't have to fight everything. Listen for once."

I do. After a moment, I feel more settled.

Faith's watching me. "Better?"

I nod.

She smiles. "My mom always says that water makes people feel better—whether it's a bath, a lake, or an ocean."

When she mentions her mom, my tears well up again. It's like those balloons inside me are floating up to push them out. I wish I knew what Ma thought would make me feel better.

"I wish I knew my ma," I say, my voice cracking. "You're so lucky."

Faith's smile tightens. She looks out at the water for a long time, then looks back at me.

"I know you think you're unlucky, Annie," she says slowly. "But let me remind you that my mom is in the hospital with cancer. Do you really think *I'm* lucky?"

"No, I didn't mean that," I say quickly.

Faith looks down at her hands. That day when she painted my nails seems like a long time ago. There are just a few traces of Tahitian Breeze left on my nails, and hers are orange now.

I swirl my toes in the lake, but the water isn't making me feel better anymore. This *conversation* isn't making me feel better. I want to be done with it, want to stick my wet feet back into my shoes and get out of here as fast as I can. I'd rather be on a roof with my sketch pad than here.

That's what I've always done when things got hard—that's what I did with the ancient Greece project girls. I walked away and never went back. But maybe that's not what I should do now.

"I need to learn to think before I speak," I say. "I know that. I'm sorry. Okay?" My words sound sharp, but it's just because I'm hurting inside.

Faith shakes her head. "Honestly, Annie? Not really."

I scrunch up my forehead, thinking. This isn't easy. But if I want to be Faith's friend, I have to try.

"The fact of me missing Ma feels really big inside me," I say. "Sometimes that feeling is so big, it pushes everything else out of the way. I think that's what happened at dinner. It was like I couldn't think of anything else."

She nods, like she's turning over my words in her mind. "I understand that—and I'm sorry about your ma. It's sad."

I'm glad she understands. I take another bite.

Faith draws in another breath, like she has something to say—but then she shakes her head. "Never mind."

I wipe my mouth. "Tell me. I can take it."

Faith looks at the water. "Sometimes it seems like you are making your ma the main point of your life, when it's something that happened a long time ago. What happened back then is *part* of who you are, sure. But does everything always have to go back to the fact that she left?"

That hurts, no lie. It pains me like a wasp sting on top of cactus needles on top of a flaming case of poison ivy. Tears pop into my eyes and threaten to fall again. Again, I think about running.

But I stay. I swish my feet in the water. I swish them and swish them until the words settle a bit. And then I realize something. Those words—even though they hurt, they might be a little bit true.

"Maybe," I say finally.

She sighs. "Can you explain why you acted so weird at dinner the other night?"

Faith's aunt Louise and Dad. The way he jumped out of his seat to wave them over. The way he looked happier than I've ever seen him. Happier than he is around Ray and me.

"Are they dating or something?" I ask.

Faith shrugs. "Would it be so bad if they were?"

I want to shout: "Yes!" It would be bad. It would be *terrible*. But I keep my mouth shut. I don't want to hurt Faith's feelings. It isn't anything personal about her aunt. Of course I know Dad deserves to be happy. I'm just afraid that I might lose him, too.

Looking out at the water, I'm so deep in my thoughts that I almost forget Faith is there.

Then something bounces gently off my cheek.

I frown, confused. Next to me, on the rock, is a piece of muffin.

But when I turn toward Faith, she just grins. She tears off another piece and launches it at me. This one plinks against my forehead.

"I'm tired of muffins," she says. "I've eaten about a thousand of each since living with Louise."

"But they're *delicious*. How can you be sick of them?"

She throws another crumb at me. "Yeah, yeah. The best in Oak Branch." But Faith is shaking her head. "Trust me. You'd get sick of them, too."

No one has ever thrown a muffin at me. It's so absurd. I scoop up the piece and toss it back at her.

Her eyebrows pop up, and her eyes go round. "Hey!"

I start cracking up. "You can dish it out, but you can't take it, huh?"

She flips another piece at me, and this means war. We hurl muffin bits at each other until they're tiny crumbs. We're laughing so hard, I can barely catch my breath.

Eventually, the pieces are too tiny to pick up anymore. I lie down on the boulder, which is warm against my back.

My cheeks ache from smiling. I can't remember the last time I laughed so hard.

Once I catch my breath, I turn sideways toward Faith. "What exactly brought that on?"

"You looked so serious! I had to do something," she says. "This summer has been serious enough. Too many what-ifs. Too many worries."

The corners of her mouth turn down. She's thinking about her mom—about her cancer. About all the question marks hanging over her family, like the balloon of questions I have about Ma.

"Faith?" I say.

She picks a crumb off her shirt before looking over at me.

"What?" she asks.

There's so much I want to say. Ma leaving is unlucky. Cancer is unlucky, too. Faith and I understand each other in that way. Nothing will ever change it.

But I can't say all that. Not without making things more serious than I want or need. Instead, I let my happiness fill me up.

I give her a big grin. "Thanks," I say. "I needed that."

She smiles wide. "Sometimes we all need a muffin thrown at us."

"You better believe it," I say.

One thing's for sure—being friends with Faith is the very best kind of luck.

CHAPTER
29

But why not, Gloria?" I ask.

The festival is a few days away. Ray and I still aren't talking. The floats are all close to finished, except Logan & Son's, which I work on every day. I've been telling Gloria about the festival for weeks. She sounded interested before but today says she has no interest in going.

I lean across my open cardboard box to give Otto a few ear scratches. He's sprawled out on my green sweatshirt again.

"Don't forget," I mutter. "I'm going to want that one back. It's my favorite."

Otto rolls onto his back and winks at me. It's hard to resist that face.

I shake my head. "Back to the festival," I say. "Why don't you want to go?"

"Humph," Gloria says. "Don't like noise, don't like people. And I sure don't like crowds of noisy people."

Otto sighs like he can read my mind. I think about the many Gloria Crumbs. The disco queen didn't mind crowds and the flight attendant probably didn't, either. There has to be something I can say to convince her.

"It won't be all that noisy," I argue. "The parade is going to loop around downtown and then finish up right here at the park across the street from your house. There will be music at the band shell, too."

Gloria's eyebrows press together. "And food?"

"*Really* good food," I answer. "Barbecue and hot dogs, kettle corn and lemonade and cookies."

"And dancing?" Gloria asks.

I nod. "Dancing, too."

"Pish," she says, like she's going to make another list of things she doesn't like. But instead she's quiet, looking down at her lap. Finally, she nods at her arm.

"Can't dance much with this thing," she says quietly.

My insides twist with guilt. I can't stand the idea of her missing out on something because of her broken arm. That would mean it was all my fault. Besides, I really want her to come.

"Maybe your cast will be off by then."

She sighs. "Not very likely. Besides, no one wants a crabby old lady there."

"Wait a minute—" I start.

"Don't argue!" she says crossly. "I know I'm a crabby old lady."

"Oh," I say. "I'm not arguing about that."

She raises her eyebrows. "You're not?"

I shake my head. "Are you kidding? I'm no mealy-mouthed sycophant kiss-up. And you are most definitely crabby and old."

Gloria's mouth presses into a line.

"No offense," I add.

"None taken," she says primly.

"But you aren't *just* anything. You're also a disco queen," I say. "Not to mention a world-traveling adventurer. I saw the pictures. Those Gloria Crumbs would say yes to a festival without thinking twice."

The corners of her mouth turn up. "Hmm. Well. *Well!*"

I can't believe I've turned Gloria Crumb speechless. It is one of my greatest accomplishments.

I bite my lip. "If I can figure out a way, will you come?"

"Fine," she says. *"Fine."*

My mind starts working in overdrive. I've got to get her there, even though it won't be easy. She deserves to be the Gloria doing her moves in the middle of a cheering crowd. The Gloria who grins as bright as the sun. If only there was a way to make it so her broken arm didn't matter one bit.

Then I start to get an idea.

CHAPTER
30

The barn bustles with activity.

It's the day before the parade. The radio volume is turned all the way up. Mostly, people are putting on finishing touches—a fabric flower here, a spray of glitter there. JoJo and The Earl occasionally take a dance break and twirl around like it's their own personal dance floor. H. Diggity set up an entire spread of hot dogs, toppings, and big containers of lemonade.

Two of the floats need a lot of work—the one for Logan & Son and the one for the town council. I think their float might be in slightly worse shape than ours. Grant and Tyler have a grand plan to construct some kind of waterfall, which they started building approximately five minutes ago.

I look at the Logan & Son float and sigh. I've done my best, but I'm not sure it's enough. I built the words like

Ray's plan except I scaled them smaller. My maple trees are lopsided but pretty. My moths are fat and furry—thanks to JoJo—but I wish I'd had the chance to make more.

But I try to look on the bright side. Overall, the effect is good. Hanging from the branches are keys, bolts, rakes, and snow shovels I've made. I have not been shy about using glitter, so they'll sparkle in the sun. And as soon as I wrap the trees in twinkle lights, they'll glow when the sun goes down, too. All I need is a ladder.

I look around the barn and spot the ladder lying on the ground near where Grant and Tyler are working. I sigh. Tyler's the last person I want to see, but I know that I need it to wrap the lights. I head over to them.

"Can I use that?" I ask.

Grant shrugs. "We're done with it."

I pick it up and start to walk away, hauling it behind me. But Tyler follows. He lifts the end of the ladder so it isn't dragging anymore.

I wheel around. "I don't need your help."

Tyler raises his eyebrows. "What did I ever do to you?"

"Like you really don't know," I say.

But he looks at me blankly. This only makes me more annoyed. Here I am, spending my whole summer with Gloria and Otto, and Tyler doesn't know he was at least partly responsible.

"You dared me to Ding-Dong Ditch Gloria," I say in a low voice.

"Oh." He nods. "That."

"Yes, *that*. And that's what made her fall. I thought you knew."

He squints at me. "I did wonder why you never came back. And I guess I thought it was strange that we were helping at that house."

"Well, now you know. Don't tell anyone, though," I say. "I've spent this whole summer trying to make up for it."

I expect him to drop his end of the ladder, but he doesn't. He helps me carry it to the other side of the barn and then sets it up.

"Where do you want this?"

"That's fine," I say. "You can go now."

Tyler sighs. "I really don't know what your problem is. But I'm not going to let you get up on this ladder without someone holding the bottom."

I open my mouth to argue, but he stops me.

"For *safety*," he says. "Weren't you just talking about Gloria falling and how much it messed her up?"

He has me there. But still—I don't know if I can trust him. I look at him warily.

He sticks out his hand like he wants me to shake it.

"I'm sorry," he says. "I never would have dared you to ring her bell if I thought she might get hurt. Okay?"

I take a moment to think, and then I nod. "Okay."

We shake hands, which feels embarrassing—too formal somehow. But it also feels like it settles something important.

He grins. "Where should I stand?"

I point at the first tree. Once the ladder is stable, I climb it.

I would never admit it, but I work faster with Tyler's help. Surprisingly, he is very particular about the best way to wrap the lights—I guess he helps his mom do the holiday decorations at their house. He makes me come down from the ladder so he can run for a roll of tape. He shows me how to anchor them and how to wrap them to get the effect I want.

This is the thing about Tyler, though. He talks the *entire* time. First he tells me he's in summer school because his grades were so bad last year, they almost kept him back. I didn't know that. Then he tells me about how his older brothers are superstars at football and lacrosse, but the thing he really wants to do is music.

He scrunches his forehead. "Do you want me to take a turn wrapping the tree? You can hold the ladder for a while."

My arms are starting to ache from the wrapping, so I agree. He climbs up the ladder, still chattering away about his plans to DJ for the dance party after the parade.

He wraps a branch as he talks. "I have my whole play-list organized except the very first song."

I frown. "If you already have a playlist, don't you have the first song, then?"

He shakes his head. "The first song is special. It has to be something people will remember."

I think about music—how much it's been a part of these nights in the barn. How even though I'm tired right now, the doo-wop of voices makes me feel happy. I think about Gloria grooving to her roller disco. And suddenly, I know what to do.

"Tyler," I say. "I have an idea for that first song."

He listens to me, and as he does, his smile spreads wide across his face—from one freckly ear to the other.

CHAPTER 31

Even though Dad's stressed about the festival, he understood when I explained the special errand I needed help with.

We load the back of his truck and drive the short distance to Gloria's. When we pull up, Albert comes over to help. After a few moments, a man wanders over. He's holding Fabian on his shoulders.

"I'm Paul," says the man.

"Hi, Paul," I say. "Hi, Fabian."

Fabian frowns at me the whole time Dad and Albert are unloading the truck.

"Careful," I say. "Don't mash the flowers. Don't scrape the glitter. Don't squash anything."

They do their best, but a few adjustments are required anyway—the de-mashing, un-scraping, de-squashing kinds of adjustments.

Together, the five of us go up to Gloria's front door. A lot has changed since the first time I was here. The whole yard has been raked. The flower beds have been weeded and are full of pink petunias. The shutters and mailbox have been rehung. And the front door is a sunny yellow, with no layers of paint peeking through.

I hear a scrabbling of nails on the floor. But instead of an angry bark, Otto announces our arrival with a happy woof.

"Good morning," Albert calls through the screen door.

"I don't see what's so good about it," Gloria says.

I shake my head, but I'm grinning. Otto's grinning, too.

"Come on, Gloria," Albert wheedles. "We have to show you something. I brought some of your friends."

"Pish. I don't have any friends," Gloria mutters. But I can hear her getting out of her chair and shuffling toward the door.

Albert steps to the side so she can see.

She blinks like she doesn't believe her eyes.

"Look what Annie made for you," Albert says.

"What have you done?" she asks.

I point at my creation. "So you can come to the parade. What do you think?"

Her fierce eyes glint. I can't tell if it's a good kind of glinting or not.

I grasp the handles of the wheelchair and whirl it around so she can get a 360-degree view. It looks amazing—a whole lot better than it did when Dad used it last year for his broken leg.

There's no hint of industrial gray on Gloria's wheelchair. Now every inch is covered in layers of fringe, streamers, and glitter. I even attached rows of pink and yellow pom-poms, in honor of the rosy maple moth. And I added her rainbow socks on the back with a mini-disco-ball ornament.

Gloria is silent.

"Oh!" I say. "I almost forgot."

I reach under the chair and push a button. Strands of twinkle lights glow.

"So it will be pretty after dark, too," I explain. "In my humble opinion, it's impossible to go wrong with twinkle lights."

But the longer she is quiet, the more I think that I did go wrong. Maybe it's too much glitter. Maybe it's too much sparkle. Maybe it's too much, *period*. I shift from one foot to the other.

"The decorations are removable," I explain. "I thought they would be right for a disco queen, but I can take them off."

"Take them off," she echoes.

I let out a jagged breath. Tears well in my eyes. I thought I could do this one thing right. I knew a wheelchair would be *helpful*, but I wanted to make it *special*. I thought she'd love it, but I was wrong. What else is new?

My shoulders slump. "Okay. I'll take them all off. You can still use the wheelchair if you want. I thought you might like it."

Gloria shakes her head as if to clear it. "I don't *like* it, my darling girl. I love it."

Darling girl? I wonder if I need to clean out my ears. But by the smile on her face, she means it. Dad looks proud. Albert and Paul beam. Baby Fabian chortles, kicking his legs with glee.

Gloria takes a seat, and Albert spins her around the driveway.

I guess even unlucky stars shine sometimes.

PART FIVE

From the Collected Drawings of Annie P. Logan

Dimensions: 8.5" × 11" (graph paper)

CHAPTER
32

With a lot of waving (unexpectedly, Fabian has turned into a champion waver), Dad and I leave Gloria's and head back through downtown.

"We better take your truck over to the barn," I say.

Dad winces. "Sorry, Annie. I know the float didn't come together. I've been so preoccupied with the store not doing well—and planning for the festival took up a lot more time than I thought it would."

I shake my head. "It's no problem, Dad. I handled it."

Dad raises his eyebrows. "Yourself?"

I shrug. "I had some help from Faith and JoJo. And from Tyler, a little."

Dad grins. "Full of surprises today, huh?" His smile feels as warm as the sun.

"I'm glad you're getting to be friends with Faith," he says as we pull into the barn.

"Me too," I say. "Are you . . . um . . . getting to be *friends* with her aunt Louise?"

After the words are out, I regret them. I'm not ready to talk to Dad about this.

Dad shuts off the engine. His cheeks are red. "I was meaning to talk to you and your brother about that—"

"There's Faith!" I say. I hop out of the car and slam the door.

She runs to me, squealing.

"My mom is getting out of the hospital this week," she says. "It could be as early as Monday!"

"Yay!" I shout, and we're jumping up and down and yelling and Faith is crying a little bit, too.

It was hard deciding which float to ride on. I worked on so many and each is special in its own way. But when JoJo mentioned that their float needed helpers to throw root beer candy into the crowd, Faith and I signed up right away.

JoJo hands us each a bulging paper sack. "Throw them into the crowd by the handful. There's more tucked away under the table, so don't be shy. And you two sample as much as you want. Don't come back with any candy, you hear? I want it all gone!"

Faith and I giggle as we each unwrap a candy. It's hard to argue with JoJo.

Before we know it, the floats are all in a line and ready to go. The parade is about to begin.

"It's time to do this," The Earl says from behind the wheel of his pickup. "Ready?"

"Ready!" we answer.

The Earl salutes us as we climb aboard. I've stood on every float in this barn and know them all inside and out. I could tell you which float is the most solid (JoJo & The Earl's) and which one is being held together on the inside with duct tape (the town council's). I could tell you which one is prettiest (Lulu's) and which is most detailed (Quinn's Market's). But my favorite is Logan & Son's. Maybe because it's a little bit like Dad and Ray and also a little bit like me.

At first, it's strange how slow the floats are traveling. It almost feels as if we're barely moving at all. But as we reach the crowds, the pace feels just right. I see faces I know and faces I don't know. I see young people and old people. Families with little kids and grandparents with grandchildren. I see hair of every color, faces of every skin tone, and bodies of all different shapes and sizes.

The little kids clap and laugh when they see the Binky Bunnies costumed characters riding on the Oak Branch Books float. And everyone screams when they realize that Tyler and Grant are riding the town council float, carrying water blasters and soaking the crowd.

Little kids ooh and aah when they see the dry ice floating from the coffee mug. And everyone cheers when they realize Faith and I are throwing candy.

Faith leans toward me. "Too bad we aren't throwing muffins."

I just laugh.

It's weird—I used to see myself as all alone. I used to think no one understood me. But up here, the perspective is different. Somehow, I see it all more clearly.

The floats have their stories and so do the people who made them. And every nail I hammered and tissue paper I glued meant that I became part of these stories as well.

This festival may have started out as a way to show Oak Branch is better than Mountain Ring. Maybe we are; maybe we aren't. We are duct tape and water blasters, a steaming mug of tea, and a hardware store my grandpa built. We are pink and yellow moths, a whole pile of glitter and glue, and a barbecue restaurant that grew from true love.

We are Oak Branch. We may have the bad luck of living near fancy Mountain Ring, but we also have the good luck of being ourselves. The good luck of the best mountain views. Of food made from kindhearted people. Of bookstores lined with incredible stories. And the good luck of the best hardware store that ever was, is, or will be. Maybe the good luck we have is enough.

CHAPTER
33

After the floats are set up on the grass around the band shell and all the vehicles have left the area, the festival officially opens. Faith's working the first shift at the Lulu's booth, so we make plans to meet up after.

The food all looks and smells amazing. I'm already deciding if I want pulled pork from JoJo & The Earl's or a hot dog with all the fixings from H. Diggity.

I'm wandering around from booth to booth. I wasn't part of this planning, so I didn't understand how many fun things there would be. There's rosy maple moth face painting at the insurance booth. There are stuffed animals so kids can do pretend dental exams. And a dunk tank set up at the town council booth.

There's even a booth for Logan & Son with a big crowd of kids wearing safety glasses. I look closer and realize it's a maker space—what Ray described back when we were painting the band shell. It's stocked with pieces of scrap wood and plenty of tools. Ray is helping a kid glue something to his project. He catches my eye and looks away.

We may be in a fight and he may hate my guts, but he's still my brother.

"This is amazing," I tell him. "Did you plan all this?"

Instead of his usual one-sided smile, he grins all the way across. "I want to show everyone that Logan and Son can design and build these for houses and businesses. I was at Tyler's last week, and Mayor Barnes said they wanted to add something to draw people to the library. I told him my idea for the maker space. It's going to show people that we aren't just a regular hardware store."

I look at the kids. They're all having a blast hammering and sawing alongside their parents.

"You're good at this," I say. I mean it.

"Thanks," he says. "Mayor Barnes said some nearby towns might want the same thing, so I'm hoping we can expand it."

It's weird. Usually this would make me feel jealous of Ray. I'd think about how perfect he is and how all the good stuff happens to him. But today, I just feel happy.

"That's part of what Dad and I have been talking about so much," he says. "We weren't trying to leave you out."

"Listen," I say. "I'm sorry about before."

Ray looks sheepish. "Me too."

When I hear this, I let out a breath I didn't know I was holding.

"I shouldn't have been rude to people trying to help," I say.

"I shouldn't have said you were selfish," Ray answers.

I don't want to tell him he may have had a point, so instead I shrug.

"It's something I'm working on," I say.

He nods, and I think he understands.

Coming up the aisle are Albert, Paul, baby Fabian, and, of course, Gloria. Her wheelchair sparkles in the sun. She beams up at me.

"Are you all having fun at the festival?" I ask.

Albert bounces Fabian. "Absolutely."

"We're heading to Oak Branch Books," says Paul. "Want to join us?"

Gloria sighs dramatically. "Heaven knows that baby needs to see his Dinky Doodads. Not that he'll ever remember it."

"Binky Bunnies," Paul corrects her.

I wonder if Gloria mixed up the name by accident, but then she winks at me.

"Hmph," she says. "Pish."

"I have an idea." Albert speaks in a careful tone. "Annie could take you around a bit, Aunt Gloria, and maybe we could all meet up after Fabian has his Binky Bunny time."

I'm already nodding, and Gloria doesn't argue—from her, that's the equivalent of shouting, "Hooray!"

I wheel Gloria past the different booths.

"Are you hungry?" I ask.

"Too early," she says.

"Thirsty?"

"Not really."

I pause. "Want to get your face painted like a rosy maple moth?"

She gives me a withering look. I try not to laugh.

"Well, *hello* there!"

I look up and find myself staring right into the eyes of my social studies teacher, who is carrying a giant plush moth.

I gulp. "Hello, Ms. Palumbo."

Ms. Palumbo looks from Gloria to me and then back to Gloria. I don't know what's swaying more—her earrings or the moth's antennae.

Ms. Palumbo beams. "I'm guessing you're Annie's mentor. She told us all about you, but I'm sorry, I don't quite remember your name. It had to do with . . . potatoes?"

I hold my breath. Gloria scowls at Ms. Palumbo, a sour look on her face. "Gloria Crumb."

Ms. Palumbo makes a fluttering motion with her fingers. "Now it's coming back to me. Franco-Hungarian, was it?"

I clear my throat. "Dutch-Romanian, right, Gloria?"

There's a long moment where Gloria squints at me. I waggle my eyebrows, which is the universal sign for "please agree with whatever I say."

"Something like that," she says eventually. "Except I'm not anyone's mentor."

Ms. Palumbo's eyebrows arch. "But it's so lovely that you've taken Annie under your wing, right at her time of blossoming."

Gloria opens her mouth, then snaps it shut. Sweat trickles down my neck.

"You mustn't sell yourself short, Mrs. Crumb."

I wait for Gloria to argue. About being my mentor. About being called *Mrs. Crumb*. About the word "blossoming," which, frankly, I wouldn't blame her for doing.

Gloria opens her mouth, and I brace myself.

"Annie is a delight. I'm proud to have her under my wing. Even if it's a broken wing at the moment," she says, indicating her cast.

I'm in shock.

Ms. Palumbo is eating it up. Gloria grins, agreeing with everything Ms. Palumbo says.

And when my social studies teacher finally walks away, Gloria clutches my arm. Then she begins to laugh. She gasps and snorts and turns bright red. I begin to worry that she might slide right out of her chair. But eventually she stops.

"Annie girl," she wheezes. "You should have seen your face. *Blossoming!* Who even says that?"

I laugh. "A mealymouthed sycophant, that's who."

Gloria shakes her head. "Your Ms. Palumbo is a real piece of work."

"She means well," I say. "I think."

Gloria's eyes twinkle. "Now you really owe me."

"I do?"

Gloria nods. "The whole story, start to finish."

So we find a table, and I tell her everything. But first I buy us two iced teas—not too bitter, not too sweet. But just right.

CHAPTER 34

The sunset is spectacular—bands of pink and yellow streak across the sky. With perfect timing, the evening is cooling down right in time for the dance party.

"The sky matches the rosy maple moths," Faith says.

Grant bumps her arm. "Did you know that a group of moths is called an eclipse?"

She catches my eye and grins, then turns back to him. I know she's hoping to dance with him tonight. I hope that for her, too.

I check my drawstring backpack for the hundredth time, but it's right on my back like it's been all day. I have everything I need.

"Uh, Annie?" Tyler asks, voice cracking. "Can we go over the plan again?"

I look at him. He's about three shades paler than usual and seems quieter, too. He keeps wiping his sweaty hands on his shorts. His first big gig as a DJ and he doesn't want to mess up.

"Tell me about the whole playlist if you want," I say, and he looks relieved.

He pulls out his phone and launches into a long explanation as to why he picked the songs he did. I just nod and say "oh?" every so often.

Finally, the sky is dark. It's time. Tyler heads over to the stage. I make my way over to Gloria, who is in her wheelchair next to Albert, Paul, and Fabian. By the time I reach her, Tyler's dad has the microphone and is welcoming everyone to the dance party.

"In a little bit, we'll announce the winners for most creative float and booth," says Mayor Barnes. "But now it's time to dance!"

There's scattered applause, and then Tyler starts to play the music. I lean down to talk to Gloria.

"Are you ready?" I ask her.

She frowns. "Ready for what?"

But then she hears it. We all do. The heavy, pulsating beat of a disco song thumps through the air.

Tyler talks smoothly into the microphone, all traces of nervousness gone. "We have a very special guest tonight. You might even say . . . she's *royalty*."

The crowd murmurs, glancing around.

"Everybody," Tyler continues, "please put your hands together for the queen of the roller disco herself, Ms.

Gloria Crumb!" And with that, he hits the button for the disco ball, and it starts to spin.

"That's our cue, Gloria!" I push her chair onto the floor and spin her. Everyone claps and cheers, then comes out on the dance floor. Tyler found a perfect first song.

Albert and Paul join us. Fabian's in the front carrier on Paul's chest, kicking his sturdy legs and wearing a small pair of noise-canceling headphones. Faith and Grant find their way over to us, and Grant is moonwalking, which isn't even from the right era, but nobody cares. Ray is here, too—as it turns out, he is not a terrible dancer. I had no idea.

Of course, the star of the night is the queen of roller disco herself, Gloria Crumb. Even in a wheelchair with a broken arm, she shimmies and wiggles, managing to dance up a storm. We all take turns with her wheelchair. Her eyes are bright and shining.

I spin around and catch sight of Dad trying to twirl Louise. I'm not going to lie: there's a pull in my chest that hurts. But after a while, it fades some. I shake my head slowly, turning back to the group. Dad is going to need to polish those moves. He's a little rusty.

Albert and Paul take turns holding Fabian, and I even hold him once so they can dance together. Of course Fabian grabs a handful of my hair and pulls as hard as he can. That baby has it out for me, but some babies are like that. I like him anyway.

We dance for an hour or more. Alicia, Nailah, and Emily are here. JoJo and The Earl, too. Even Ms. Palumbo, her earrings shaking to the music. The whole time, the light from the disco ball spins around us like we're surrounded by stars.

Eventually, the songs slow and the music fades.

"Hello, hello, hello," Tyler says into the microphone in a much deeper voice than usual. I can see his grin from here. He's absolutely *loving* being a DJ. "Everyone, please put your hands together to welcome JoJo McCoy to the stage. Not only does she make the most legendary pies of all time, today she has some very special announcements you won't want to miss."

JoJo walks onto the stage, holding several envelopes. She's beaming. "Thank you, Tyler! Welcome, everyone, to the first annual Rosy Maple Moth Festival in good old Oak Branch. We hope you're having a nice time in our little town."

The crowd roars, everyone stomping their feet.

"Now," she says. "We'll get back to dancing in a minute, but first we have some recognizing to do. I'll make it quick. For the most creative float, the prize goes to . . . the town council for their interactive waterfall!"

Mayor Barnes comes onstage to take the certificate. He jokes like he's going to take the microphone again, but

JoJo pulls it out of reach. If Mayor Barnes starts talking, we could be here all night.

"For the booths, the most creative award goes to . . . Logan and Son!"

Ray's head jerks up in surprise.

I cheer and stomp my feet. "Go, Ray! You did great."

He smooths his shirt and goes onto the stage, allowing himself a smile when JoJo hands him the certificate.

"We have one more note of recognition for this evening," she says.

I watch Fabian, whose eyelids are starting to droop. It's a late night for a little baby. Paul leans down and pretends to nibble Fabian's cheek, and Fabian pats Paul's hand lazily.

"This is for an individual who has truly gone above and beyond," JoJo says. "The words that come to mind are 'helpful,' 'community service,' 'compassion.' The spirit of volunteerism."

Gloria is pretending to play peekaboo with Fabian. He looks at her warily.

"We're truly proud of this young person, who has spent her entire summer volunteering."

I yawn, starting to feel tired now that I'm standing still. It's been a long day. I hope the music will start again soon.

"Will you please come to the stage—" JoJo pauses dramatically. "Miss. Annie. P. Logan!"

I freeze.

"Come on, Annie! Are you out there?" JoJo peers at the crowd.

I can't believe my ears.

It feels like the world is spinning. Albert pats me on the back. The clapping is so loud.

Gloria grins. "What are you waiting for, girl? Get up there and get your prize!"

I walk on jelly legs to the stage.

JoJo, smiling, holds up the certificate. I see my name in curving script.

But I don't reach for it—I'm not who they think I am. I didn't rescue Gloria—didn't volunteer out of the goodness of my heart. How can I accept an award that reminds me of the bad luck I bring to everyone I know?

JoJo's eyebrows knit together in concern. "Annie?"

In the audience, Dad's cheering, too. I'm not Unlucky Annie anymore. I'm not the one who made Ma leave. It's just me. Just Annie. It's all I ever wanted.

But my glance catches on Gloria, who is highly visible thanks to her tricked-out wheelchair. She's cheering for me, face in a wide-open smile.

All summer I've felt a pit of guilt in my stomach. Right now I feel like I've fallen into a bottomless hole.

JoJo tries to put the paper in my hand, but I pull away.

"I can't accept this. I'm sorry."

I run away into the starless night.

CHAPTER
35

A nnie! Annie!"

I hear Dad behind me, but I don't slow down.

He's faster than I am, though, and it doesn't take long for him to catch up.

"What's going on? Why did you run away?"

"I don't want to talk about it," I say, crossing my arms.

Even in the dark, I can see the tips of his ears flame red. "Well, you're going to!"

I stop and look at him, shocked.

"I'm not going anywhere," he says. "I'll wait right here until you tell me."

Hot tears pop in my eyes, and I scrub them with the back of my hand. I don't want to cry.

He watches me silently.

"That day when Gloria fell," I start and then stop again. "There was a little more to that story."

Dad raises his eyebrows.

I clear my throat. "Maybe someone dared me to ring her doorbell and run away."

Disappointment shadows Dad's face. He shakes his head.

I bite my lip. "I didn't *ring* the doorbell—I changed my mind. But it was too late. Otto started barking, Gloria came to the door, and she fell."

Dad sighs. "I'm more disappointed about the lying than anything else."

I shake my head quickly. "I didn't lie about it, not really."

Dad squints a skeptical look at me. It reminds me of the look on Faith's face when we sat on the boulder. I need to try harder.

"I didn't *lie*," I say slowly. "But I admit I wasn't all that truthful, either."

He sighs deeply. He's irritated, exasperated. He doesn't understand.

"I'm really disappointed," he says.

"Of course you are," I say. "Like always."

Dad's eyebrows draw together, forehead wrinkling. "Annie, I—"

"Just once," I say, voice shaking. "I wish I felt like you wanted me. Annie. That you weren't sad that I wasn't more like Ray. That you weren't wishing this whole time that Ma had taken me with her."

He opens his mouth to speak, but I don't want to hear it.

"This summer, for the first time, I felt like you were finally proud of me," I say. "I'm sorry it was all a lie."

Dad freezes. A muscle in his jaw tenses.

I brace myself for his anger. I feel it coming. This is it—he's finally going to boil over after all these years. He'll say those things I've been so afraid to hear.

But Dad doesn't explode. Instead, he slumps.

His head tilts down so far, I can't see his face. He stays like that for a moment, rubbing his forehead again and again, right where the worry wrinkles usually are. But when he looks up, he isn't angry. His eyes shimmer. Dad is *crying*.

"Annie," he says in a choked voice.

He opens his arms and takes a step toward me. A memory flits across the back of my brain like a brightly colored butterfly—how I'd run to him after he came home from work, how he'd scoop me skyward.

I pause.

Seven years of questions float in my brain like balloons—seven years of missing Ma, of feeling like I'm on my own. I want to let those balloons go; I really do. But I don't know how. Those balloons take up so much space inside me, there's almost no room for anything else.

Every thought of being unlucky, every question about what happened, every faded memory of Ma.

But those balloons are empty.

I take a step toward him. He sees me coming and meets me halfway. When he grabs me in his hug, his arms are warm and strong, just like I remember. He's saying something against the top of my head, but I can't make out the words. He's crying. And he's whispering the same thing again and again.

"Always, Annie," he says. "I'm always so proud of you."

I stretch my arms wide and hug him back.

CHAPTER
36

Dad and I don't return to the party. Instead, he takes me home. Tomorrow I'll have a lot of explaining to do—to JoJo and The Earl, to Tyler, to Grant and Faith, to Albert and Paul, and, most of all, to Gloria. But right now, I really need my dad.

He heads to the kitchen, saying he'll make us some mint tea, the organic kind he keeps in a special tin. I switch on the lamp with the green glass base, the twin of the one I smashed accidentally so many years ago. After a few minutes, he returns with a mug for each of us.

"Where's Ray?" I ask.

"He'll stay at Tyler's tonight."

We sit on the couch, both sipping our tea. The mint clears my head, and the honey is soothing.

Dad clears his throat. "Where did you get the idea that I'm not proud of you?"

I squirm. "We don't have to talk about that."

"We do," he says simply.

I curl my fingers around the mug, letting its warmth soak into my hands. "You and Ray are the same. Ma and I are the same."

Dad sets down his tea. "Go on."

"You kind of light up around Ray. You always have things to talk about. Like running or building things or . . . oatmeal."

Dad frowns faintly. "You think your brother and I talk about oatmeal?"

I shake my head. "You both *like* oatmeal is my point. I don't. I'm always the odd one out."

"I see," Dad says.

But now that I've started, I don't want to stop. "Ma always said I was born under an unlucky star. Maybe it's true, Dad. I feel like I never get things right. Bad things happen to me all the time."

He sighs. I wait for him to tell me I'm wrong, but he doesn't.

"Sometimes I think I'm the reason Ma left," I say. "Me and my unlucky stars."

"Unlucky stars," Dad scoffs. "I wish she'd never filled your head with that."

I cross my arms. "At least she filled my head with *something*. You never talk to me. You never talk about *her*."

He nods slowly. Usually, it's like my words bounce right off him. But now it's as if I can see them sinking in.

"Okay," he says finally. "What do you want to know?"

My eyes widen. It's what I've been waiting for my whole life.

"Really?" I ask.

"Really," he says.

I better act now before this window of opportunity closes. "For starters, you could go ahead and tell me everything. What was she like? Why did she leave?"

He smiles. "She was beautiful. You look so much like her. She loved poetry and languages. Was learning Italian, just in case. In case of what, I always wanted to ask, but never did. She'd never let me squash a spider. Said it was bad luck."

I look straight down at my mug. I'm afraid if I breathe wrong, he'll stop talking. I need him to go on.

"Without a doubt, she was the most fascinating person I'd ever met," he continues. "Always with her own way of doing things. Opera dinners, where we dressed up nice and listened to a recording. Or buying new foods at the grocery store, even if we didn't know how to cook them. Like artichokes."

"I love artichokes," I tell him.

"Me too," he says, eyes twinkling.

"She did things in a big way," I say.

He nods. "Exactly."

We sit still like that, both wearing quiet grins. I feel closer to Dad than I have in a long time. Maybe more than I ever have.

I'm about to say so when I realize that Dad's smile is fading.

"There were other things too—things that weren't so fun." His voice is low, more like a rumble than a whisper.

I feel my insides shrink up. Half of me is afraid to hear it. But the other half is hungry—starving—for every tiny detail.

The hungry half wins. "Like what?" I ask.

His eyes turn down at the corners. "Sometimes she'd get an itch to be on the road. In the middle of the night, she'd hop in the car and drive for hours, not even leaving a note. I'd wake up in the morning, not knowing where she was."

I squeeze the handle of my tea mug. "She liked adventures," I say, and I can hear the stubbornness in my voice.

"It was scary," Dad says. "Especially after you and Ray were born."

I frown, puzzled. "Why is that?"

Dad blows out a deep breath. "The drives got longer and less predictable. One morning right after you were born, she called me from Montgomery, Alabama. You and your brother were in the backseat. Until the phone woke me, I didn't even know you were gone."

I think about little Fabian and how scared Albert and Paul would be if they didn't know where he was. When I imagine it that way, Ma's drives don't seem quite as fun.

Dad taps the side of his mug with his index finger. "After I realized you were two whole states away, I broke down crying. That's what it took for her to understand how worried I was. She finally agreed to go to the doctor."

I hide my face behind my tea mug. I don't know which I find more shocking—this story, which I've never heard before. Or the idea of Dad breaking down in tears.

"It took a while, but eventually she was diagnosed with something called bipolar, which is a mental illness. The best way I can describe it is that it was like she was fighting a constant battle inside her. She had a lot of highs and lows. A week being happy—so full of energy, she could barely sleep. Then a couple weeks of feeling so sad and hopeless, where she could barely get out of bed. No real pattern, no rhyme or reason. Up or down, with nothing in between."

Dad takes another sip of tea. "This is the thing, though: big moments—the adventures, like you said—might be fun and exciting. But real life is lived on a smaller scale. String enough of those little moments together and that's what makes something big—a marriage. A family. A life. If you're always chasing something grand, life can start to feel empty."

I turn the words over in my mind. "Is that why she left?"

Dad sighs. "After the diagnosis, I thought everything would be okay. But staying healthy wasn't easy. The medicine flattened her out, made her feel like she wasn't herself. She stopped taking it."

There's a frayed spot on the couch and I run my fingers over the bumpy threads. I want to ask something else, but I don't know how Dad will react.

"If she had kept taking her medicine, do you think she would have stayed?" I ask.

Dad sighs. "I don't know how to answer that. I know she loved you. And I know that a lot of the time, she was a great mom."

I nod. "Like the spaghetti bathtub dinners."

Dad shakes his head. "Those dinners were fun, but that isn't what I mean. She had this way of understanding you and your brother—just by looking at you. It was really something."

I don't know what he means. Dad glances at my face and seems to be able to read my confusion.

"I'll try to think of an example," Dad says, his forehead scrunching as he remembers. "When you were a toddler, you sometimes held your breath until you passed out."

My eyebrows pop up. "I fainted? You never told me that."

The corner of his mouth turns up. "Ma looked for the pattern. She realized that it happened when you got upset. It was like your emotions were too big for your little body. So she would watch you to anticipate those reactions—she'd talk to you about your feelings, help you with them."

As I listen to his words, it feels like a missing piece clicking into place. I don't remember those things happening—not exactly. But it feels right to me. It helps explain why losing Ma felt like losing a piece of myself.

Dad sips his tea. "Do you remember the day that you got the scar on your hand?"

"The dog walked past Ray so it could bite me," I say. "Yet another example of my rotten luck."

Dad frowns. "That isn't what happened."

I raise my eyebrows. "It's not?"

He shakes his head. "She left Ray on the picnic blanket while she showed you a patch of wild blackberries. When she looked up, a dog was barking and growling at Ray. She set you down so she could chase the dog away, but she tripped and fell. Meanwhile, you ran straight toward that dog as fast as your little legs would carry you. You jumped in front of Ray to protect him, and that's when you got bit."

I almost drop my mug. That's not the story I thought I knew. "I *saved* Ray? Are you sure?"

Dad nods. "Other people saw it, too. No one could believe how brave you were. She was wracked with guilt. She couldn't stop thinking about what might have happened if the dog had attacked you, if you never recovered . . ." He trails off.

My brain spins. It's too much to take in.

"I think it was her fear that made her go," Dad says, voice scratching. "Fear she would do something to hurt you or Ray."

Tears prickle my eyes. "But it didn't work. Her leaving hurt us, too."

"I know it," he says. "But in her mind, I think she did it out of love."

I shake my head. It hurts to hear him say those words, even though I want them to be true.

"Love isn't someone who runs. Love is someone who stays," I tell him. "If she loved me, she would be here right now."

His eyes turn down. "She did love you, Annie. I believe she did the best she could. Sometimes that's all we get, even if it isn't fair."

I open my mouth to talk, but then I realize he isn't finished yet.

He clears his throat. "I know you think I don't understand you, and I may never understand your ideas about the stars. But it has always perplexed me that someone who has brought such joy and happiness to my life could ever think of herself as unlucky. Because, without a doubt, you and Ray have made me the luckiest man alive."

I take a deep breath. "She's never coming back, is she?"

Dad gives me a long look. "No, I don't think so, Annie."

Hearing the words feels like ripping off an old scab. It's not that I'm surprised—deep down, part of me has known that for a long time. But still, it hurts to hear Dad say it. She's never coming back.

Dad pats my hand awkwardly, like he doesn't know what to do. His forehead is scrunched with worry-wrinkles, and I realize that he's worried about me.

"I do love you and Ray," I say. "It's just that I really wanted to know her, too."

"She was someone worth knowing," says Dad. "I'm sorry you didn't get much of a chance."

That's when the tears come. I sob until I shake. I wail until I can't make another sound. I lean sideways into my dad like I'm sure he'll always be there.

CHAPTER
37

Festivals are all fun and games until the very next day when it's time to clean up.

Planning is a big job, but at least it's fun. There are pretty things to think about—like floats. Delicious things to think about—like food vendors. And logistical things to think about—like parade routes, getting the right permits, making sure everything is organized smoothly.

But getting rid of the festival is a real mess. Especially when my eyes are barely open. If I had known Dad signed us up to help, maybe I would have tried to go to sleep earlier.

Then again, maybe not. Talking to Dad was worth it.

So here we are, with the glamorous job of picking up garbage on the lawn. Ray and Tyler are on the other side of the band shell, helping load tables and chairs into pickup trucks.

"The sun is barcly up," I say.

Dad catches my eye. "That's a bit of an exaggeration."

I look around. "Okay, fine. It's an exaggeration."

"But it *is* early," he admits. No one will ever describe Dad as dramatic or exaggerating, but getting him to acknowledge this feels like a victory. He's meeting me in the middle.

It feels different between us today. Last night, my feelings were raw. I cried so hard, my eyes felt like medium-grit sandpaper. But already some of those feelings are changing—being replaced with something that is more solid, more steady.

We walk together in silence, picking up loose trash when we find it. My thoughts keep returning to the night before—to how I ran away. This afternoon, I'll talk to Gloria and explain it all. I hope she'll still be my friend after she knows the truth.

Dad and I fill up two bags. We're adding them to the pile when I hear someone shout.

"Hey! Whose dog is that?"

My thoughts turn back to the picnic in the park all those years ago—but that dog who bit my hand isn't here. Instead, I look up and see Otto running at full speed. I've never once seen him move with such purpose—he's really flying, his ears whipping behind him. Who could have ever guessed that he was made to run like this?

He makes a beeline right for me, then sits down in front of me. I reach to pet him, but he ducks his head away. He barks at me, but it's not like any bark I've ever heard.

"What's up, Otto?" Dad asks.

"He's acting really weird, Dad!"

Otto pushes his head against me.

"How did you get out?" I ask. "Gloria has got to be worried sick."

He opens his mouth with those wild, crooked teeth. I wait for him to let his tongue unfurl and roll over for a belly rub, but he doesn't. Instead he sinks those teeth into my pants leg and pulls. Otto, who's never once put his mouth on me. Otto, who would never hurt a fly. I look at Dad.

"Something's wrong." I can hear the rising panic in my voice. "Something's really wrong!"

I sprint for Gloria's house as fast as I can. Otto races ahead. Dad shouts to Ray and then is at my heels, but I'm flying. I swoop up the driveway and the front steps, pulling open the screen door, mesh gaping wide where Otto broke through.

I hope she'll be sitting in her chair like normal. I wish that I'll hear her crabbiest voice. I pray that she'll glare at me with those fierce blue eyes.

But Gloria Crumb is lying on the floor. And this time, she isn't moving.

CHAPTER
38

The ambulance takes Gloria away in a rush of sirens.

Dad, Ray, and I follow in Dad's truck. When we get to the lobby, Albert and Paul are already there, disappearing through double doors to a room in the back.

We wait and wait, but there's no news.

"I wish we knew what was happening," I say.

"I know," Dad says. He gets up to find a cup of coffee. He asks if we want anything. I think about too-sweet tea and feel like crying. I shake my head no.

A ball of twisted feelings forms in my belly. All I want is for Gloria to be okay.

Ray clears his throat. "I'm sorry about Gloria."

"She's not dead, Ray," I snap at him.

He turns pale. "Sorry."

I shake my head. "I shouldn't have snapped at you. I'm just worried about it all."

Ray nods, and that's that.

Dad returns with his coffee and a lumpy-looking scone. "These sure aren't as good as Louise's."

"I don't think these can even be put in the same category," I say, and he smiles.

A few hours pass. Eventually, Albert comes back to see us. He runs his hand through his hair. "It seems like it's going to be a while. They're running some tests."

My heart rises. "So she's alive?"

He nods once. "Alive, yes. But not responsive."

"How can we help?" Dad asks.

Albert runs his hand through his hair, which makes it stick up. He looks worried and unsure.

"We could pick up Otto," I say.

I may be imagining it, but I think I feel Dad stiffen. I look at him sideways.

"No, no," Albert says. "I'll send Paul for him."

"If you're sure," Dad says quickly.

I scowl. "Dad, can't we relax the no-pets rule? It's an emergency."

He ignores me.

"We'll message you as soon as there's news," Albert says. And then a nurse is calling his name and he's rushing off again.

I can't stop thinking about Gloria lying on the floor, not moving. I can't stop thinking about how scared and lonely Otto must feel.

We get in the truck and drive home. The only thing to do is wait.

Somehow, the day passes. I jump each time Dad's phone beeps, but there's no message from Albert. Eventually, Dad says it's bedtime and tells Ray and me to go to our rooms.

I close my bedroom door behind me. I open my sketch pad, but I don't feel like drawing. Instead I slide open the window and crawl outside on my roof.

There's a big fat moon tonight. The July air is cool and crisp. I breathe it into my lungs and try not to think of Gloria and Otto. It would be easier, I think, if I'd never known them.

Ribbons of guilt twist around my heart. I don't want to erase Gloria and Otto from the universe. I want to anchor them to it. To me.

"I take it back," I whisper.

I hear a sliding sound, and I turn my head. It's Ray. He's pushed open his window and is climbing out his bedroom window—onto the roof with me.

He sits down, hugging his knees to his chest. "I thought I'd find you here."

My mouth drops open. "Raymond K. Logan, are you really out here breaking a rule?"

He shrugs, grinning. "You don't own this roof, you know."

"*Pish.*" I say it like Gloria, which makes me feel like a whole bucket of sad-happy just rained down on me.

In the moonlight, I can see his eyebrows arch upward. "*Pish?* What in the world does that mean?"

"I'm not actually sure," I admit. "But I think it's what you say when someone is annoying you."

Ray cracks up, and I do, too. We laugh until our shoulders shake and our bellies ache. We laugh until we cry.

"Pish," he shouts. The sound bounces off my mountains and echoes back at us.

"Pish!" I howl.

"Kids?" says a low voice.

Ray and I spin toward the sound. It's Dad, standing inside my bedroom, looking out the window like he's not sure what he sees.

Ray and I look at each other. We are in such trouble.

But Dad's crouching low. He's crawling onto the roof. And when we look at his face, he's smiling.

"So," he says. "Pish?"

"Pish," Ray and I answer, nodding.

Waiting isn't easy, but at least we're together. We stay like that for hours—my family, my mountains, and the moon.

CHAPTER
39

Annie," Dad calls. "Wake up!"

"Mrph," I mumble. "Too early."

But yesterday comes flooding through my brain in a rush. Maybe there's news about Gloria. My eyes pop open, and my feet land on the floor. I'm swinging the door wide open.

Dad stands there, holding his phone in one hand. "I got a message from Albert. They want us to come to the hospital."

My eyes widen. "Did they say if she's okay?"

Dad's worry lines furrow on his forehead. "Sorry, Annie. He didn't say."

I throw on clothes and come downstairs, where Ray is already waiting. No one has oatmeal. We get in the truck.

Dad backs down the driveway. "Annie, I think you need to prepare yourself for any outcome. She might not—"

Anger flares inside me. Even though he's just giving voice to the fears of my heart, I don't want to hear it. "We don't even know what happened, Dad! Gloria is tougher than you know. I won't give up on her."

Dad pauses. "She's very old, honey. She may not have much time left."

I smack my hand on the seat. "You think she's dead, don't you?"

Dad shakes his head. "I didn't say that."

I frown. "She can't be dead, Dad. I never got the chance to tell her I'm sorry."

He doesn't say anything, just drums his hands on the steering wheel for the rest of the drive.

When we get to the hospital, Albert is in the waiting room having a cup of coffee. The skin under his eyes looks purple. It's like he's been awake all night.

He stands up as soon as he sees us. "Come with me, Annie. She's asking for you."

Never have I been so happy to hear the present tense. If Gloria is asking for me, she must be okay. I breathe out a sigh of relief.

Albert leads me to the hall outside her room. "You can go inside. I think I'm going to get more coffee."

I want to ask him to stay but he disappears before I can say a word. This is not how I thought it would go.

Gloria lies on her back in the hospital bed. Her eyes are closed. She's hooked up to monitors measuring her heartbeat and oxygen level. She looks small in the hospital bed, like a doll.

"Gloria?" I say, just above a whisper.

She opens her eyes suddenly, which makes me jump backward.

She chuckles but winces like it hurts. "Didn't mean to scare you."

I cross my arms. "You didn't scare me!"

She eyes me carefully. "Oh, yes I did."

"Maybe a little," I admit.

She chuckles again. "Now, Annie. I need to ask—why did you run off the other night, when there was an award there with your name on it?"

I sigh. We're going to get right to it, I guess.

"It would be wrong for me to accept it," I answer but then stop short. My tongue suddenly feels too big for my mouth. These words are hard to say.

Gloria frowns impatiently. "Come on, girl! Spit it out!"

"How can I get an award for saving you when I'm the one who caused your fall? Everyone thinks I was just walking by, but really I was going to ring your doorbell as a prank." I am so miserable, I can barely look at her.

Even though Gloria is weak, she glares at me so hard I can feel it in my bones. I gulp. She's surprised, disappointed. Whatever she's about to say, I deserve it.

But Gloria rolls her eyes skyward, looking for all the world like an irritated teenager. "Tell me something I don't know!"

"*What?*" I exclaim. Gloria knew? I don't understand.

She looks smug. "I had my suspicions already. But then you told me yourself that day you thought I was napping."

My mouth drops open. I think back to the day Gloria fell asleep in her chair, Otto snuggled in my sweatshirt. At least, I thought she was asleep.

"I didn't think you heard me!" I say.

She looks very pleased with herself. "I could tell I was about to hear something interesting, so I kept my eyes shut and my ears open."

I shake my head slowly. Outsmarted by Gloria Crumb.

A flicker of a smile crosses her face but then she frowns again. "Anyhow. What's that you were saying about not saving me?"

I'm confused. Did she forget? Does she need me to explain again how it was my fault? "I was going to ring the doorbell—"

Gloria shakes her head. "You may not have been there for the right reasons, but the fact remains that you *did come to my rescue*. You could have walked away."

I bite my lip. "I never would have done that."

Her eyes shine. "I already know that, Annie. Believe it or not, I have been paying attention this summer."

Her voice is gentle—not syrupy-pancake sweet, but a kind of sweet that feels real. A kind of sweet that feels like maybe I earned it a little.

She fixes me with her bright-blue gaze, letting the words sink in. "There's more than one way to save a person. You took care of me just as much as you took care of Otto. That's a different kind of saving. One I didn't know I needed."

My breath catches. Tears pop in my eyes. "But—"

"No buts!" she roars. "No nuts, no buts, no coconuts!"

"I—u-um—" I stammer.

"We used to say that in school," she says primly. "Anyhow, Annie P. Logan. I need you to claim that award. You deserve it. There are enough times in life that you'll be passed over for such things. I won't have you throwing them away."

"But—"

She eyes me. I feel my words shrink up under her glare.

"And another thing," she says. "I'm going to go into the home for old folks."

Oh no. This is exactly what I didn't want to happen.

She sees my face and shakes her head. "It's my choice. I wanted to make the decision before someone else had to do it for me."

I gulp. Gloria moving to a home and leaving Otto really is my fault. There are no two ways about it. I have to tell her everything.

"Gloria," I say. "It's my bad luck that brought this on you."

Her eyes narrow, her gaze surprisingly sharp. "You told me about this bad luck nonsense before. Something about stars, wasn't it?"

"Right," I say, but then pause for a moment. "But I got some of it wrong."

She squints at me, waiting for me to continue.

"A long time ago, a dog in the park bit me. I thought these scars proved my bad luck, but maybe that's not right," I say. "Maybe it didn't happen because I was unlucky. Maybe it happened because I was brave."

"Or," says Gloria. "Maybe you're neither. Or maybe you're both!"

She laughs when she sees my expression. "Whoever said that you could be only one thing? Haven't you been paying attention at all? I would hope, as your mentor, I would have at least taught you that."

She grins wide. The word mentor zooms me back to that day in Mr. Melendez's office. It seems like a century ago. Gloria Crumb is no Jackie Zpudzz— she's even better. She's Gloria the roller-disco queen. Gloria the adventurer. Gloria the big sister. Gloria, my friend.

I take a deep breath. "The thing is, I've believed in my bad luck for a long time. I thought it explained so much. Without my bad luck, who will I be?"

"My girl," Gloria says, eyes twinkling. "Don't look so sad. You'll figure it out. Figuring out who you are is the fun part of life."

She reaches for my hand, tracing the dots, bumps, and lines that look like a constellation.

"I'm really sorry that I made you fall," I say.

She shrugs, her eyes bright and fierce. "I don't know if we're ruled by the heavens. I've been around a long time and have never seen proof one way or the other."

She winks. "But if it's true, then these unlucky stars are the same ones that brought you to me. And I wouldn't change a thing."

She squeezes my hand. I hold on tight.

CHAPTER
40

After a while, the nurse says it's time for me to go.

Gloria says she'll see me soon.

Dad and Ray sense that I don't want to talk, and the ride home is quiet. As much as it was good to see Gloria, my thoughts are a tangled mess. There's no way to tell the future. I want her to be okay. I want her to be with Otto, but that's impossible if she's going to Shady Lane. The thought sinks my heart like a stone.

When we get home, there's a red hatchback car in our driveway. Faith is on our front porch, holding two huge bakery boxes. Louise is in the driver's seat. She smiles shyly when she sees us and rolls down her window.

"We were just going to drop off a few things on your porch," she says. "I know it was a long night."

Faith holds up the box. "We have muffins!"

Dad turns off the truck and goes over to Louise. "Come on in and visit for a while. I'm glad to see you." When she gets out of her car, he wraps her in a big hug. I'm not sure if I'm ready to be around that quite yet. I open the front door, and Faith and I go inside.

We put the box on the kitchen counter and investigate its contents. It's stacked full of deliciousness—triple-berry muffins and lemon scones, cinnamon bread and white chocolate–peach squares. And plenty of my favorite corn muffins with little cups of extra strawberry butter. Dad is making coffee and talking to Aunt Louise. Faith and I pile a plate and head upstairs. Food in bedrooms is against Dad's rules, but something tells me that he won't even notice.

Upstairs, we sit on my bed and stuff ourselves with sweets. I tell Faith everything—I explain why I ran off the way I did. Then I tell her all about seeing Gloria at the hospital.

"Gloria said she wouldn't change a thing," I tell her.

Faith looks at me carefully. "You sound like you don't believe it."

I shake my head. "I *do* believe it—she squeezed my hand so hard, I can still see the marks."

"I get it," says Faith. "You believe it for *her*. But you don't believe it for *you*."

I shrug. I don't know if I feel like talking, but Faith is still looking at me, waiting for an answer.

"My head and my heart are battling," I say.

Faith nods. "What does your head say?"

I gulp. "My head says—it would be easier if I never met them. Even if Gloria lives . . . she'll die someday, right?"

Faith's brown eyes widen. I could kick myself. Of course she's thinking about her mom. But she's not crying. Instead, she looks thoughtful.

She tilts her head sideways, speaking slowly. "That's true for everyone, though—right? Everyone dies. No one knows how much time they have left."

I shrug. "It may be true for everyone, but it seems *more* true for Gloria."

Faith breaks a white chocolate–peach square in two and hands me half. My room is quiet except for the sound of chewing.

"I felt that way a little this summer, about my mom," she says finally. "I avoided video chat, and I wasn't texting her back."

I raise my eyebrows. "What happened?"

Faith smiles, dimples popping. "She said I didn't get a choice, that I was her baby no matter what, and she needed to see me."

I wait for the balloon thoughts to crowd my brain, wishing that Ma needed to see *me* no matter what. But the thoughts don't come. Instead, I think about my friend and how hard this summer must have been. How Faith's life is lucky and unlucky mixed together. How maybe mine is, too.

"I'm glad she's coming home soon," I say. I mean it.

Faith flashes a wide grin. "Me too. I want you to meet her."

"What was it like when you talked to her again?" I ask.

Faith laughs. "First, she was mad. But we talked it out. It didn't feel good to keep myself separate from my mom. But loving people is a risk."

I turn over Faith's words in my mind. She was trying to protect herself from being hurt. But she ended up hurting her mom—and herself.

Sometimes love hurts, but I think maybe it's worth it.

CHAPTER 41

It's been almost a month since the night of the festival. The days are still warm, but they're starting to turn cool around the edges, like fall wants to let us know it's on the way.

Gloria heals. Her cast comes off. She moves to Shady Lane. Otto lives with Albert, Paul, and Fabian. I haven't seen him since that day at the park. I wish I had remembered to tell him what a brave dog he was. Maybe Albert can tell him for me.

Up until the day Gloria moved, I thought she'd change her mind. With her arm healed, she could have stayed at her house with Otto. She said no, moving was for the best—for her and for Otto, too. It scared her that he escaped, and she doesn't want it to happen again. Besides, it turns out Shady Lane has a monthly disco party. No roller skates, though, of course, which is too bad.

I visit her in the hospital. One time, I asked her what to save from her boxes.

She leaned against the pillows, smiling. "If you can find that picture of me and little Albert, I'd like that."

My mouth dropped open. In all those boxes, there was only one thing she wanted. "That's all? What about the other pictures? What about your crown?"

She shook her head. "You keep anything you want."

I asked Albert to save the crown for me. I know that it will always remind me of Gloria—not just Gloria the disco queen or Gloria the adventurer. It will remind me of all the Glorias she is and ever was. The least mealy-mouthed person I know.

The house was listed for sale before Gloria even left the hospital. Albert said it's thanks to Ray and me. With all my work going through boxes and all of Ray's work fixing up the outside, the house was in much better shape than it had been at the beginning of summer. I was glad we were helpful, but I didn't feel very glad when I saw the For Sale sign out front.

Luckily, I didn't have to see it for very long. Her house was snapped up within a week by a newlywed couple with three kittens. *Cats*, living in Otto's house! I wondered what he'd think about that.

I wonder about Otto a lot. I didn't know him very long, but I like to think we understood each other. He needed help coming into the world, and I guess I did, too.

I sure hope Albert and Paul have learned his favorite spots for belly scratches. I hope Fabian doesn't scowl too much. It might hurt Otto's feelings.

I haven't made it out to Shady Lane to see Gloria. I will, but I'm not ready yet. Because when I see her without Otto, I think the whole truth of this summer is going to hit me. I need to guard my heart a little longer, until I'm ready.

This morning, Albert is going to stop by to drop off the crown. We're just finishing breakfast when the doorbell rings.

Dad looks at me. "Aren't you going to get that?"

Before shoving my chair back from the table, I eat my last two bites of oatmeal. Believe it or not, I actually like oatmeal now. Louise showed me a little trick of adding cream and blueberries, which magically turns regular old oatmeal into something delicious.

When I answer the door, Albert is standing there. But he isn't alone.

It's the best surprise ever. I fall to my knees.

"Otto!" I say.

Otto bounds over to me, swishing his tail so hard, he practically falls over. I lean down and start giving him ear scratches. He flops over right there on the porch to show his belly.

"Look at you, out on an adventure," I say, touching his soft fur. "Such a brave dog."

As if to answer, his tongue rolls out the side of his mouth in a classic Otto grin.

Ray joins us on the porch. "Otto's here for a visit? Great!"

Dad shakes his head. "He's not here for a visit."

I cross my arms. Of course, I should have known. Dad and his rules.

"Please, Dad," I say. "Just a short one. I've missed him so much."

Otto stretches his paws out contentedly.

Dad sighs. "Come here, Otto. Let me have a look at you."

Otto is in a cooperative mood. He stands up and shakes himself. Then he trots over to Dad and sits at his feet.

Dad looks down at him. "What a funny-looking brute."

Otto's tail wags, like he has no idea he's being criticized.

"Dad!" I say. "That's rude."

"Hmm," Dad says skeptically. "He sure has a lot of teeth."

"He's the least ferocious dog of all time," I tell him. "He wouldn't hurt a fly, would you, Otto?"

Dad reaches down to scratch behind Otto's ears. "So hairy. I bet he's prone to tangles."

"Easily fixed by a little brushing," I say.

Dad rubs Otto's chin. "What's the deal with these eyes that point in different directions?"

I sniff. "Pish. He's distinctive. *Unique.*"

Dad laughs, straightening up. He looks at Albert and nods. "All right."

My eyes get round. "You mean it—he can visit?" My mind fills with all the places I want to take him. I can show him my room and the backyard. I want to walk him along the stream. Maybe I can find an old tennis ball and teach him how to fetch.

Dad's face is unreadable. "He can't visit."

Oh. My heart caves in on itself. I bury my face in my hands. I want to block out the whole world.

"Annie," Albert says softly. "Listen to your dad."

I wipe my eyes and look at Dad. My fists turn into tight balls. I'm ready to give him a piece of my mind. I'm ready to tell him how unfair he is. I'm ready to—

Dad smiles so wide, his eyes crinkle up.

"Otto can't visit," he says slowly. "Because he's already home."

I freeze. I must be hearing things.

"What?" shouts Ray. "Really?"

"We think he misses Annie," Albert says. He holds up something in a familiar shade of green.

"My sweatshirt!" It's covered in Otto's hair.

"He won't sleep without it," Albert says. "We didn't understand why. Then, the other day, I tried to wash it, and he cried and cried. Then Paul looked inside and saw your name."

"But, Dad," I say. "What about your rules?"

Dad's eyes twinkle. "Some things are bigger than rules."

I sink my hands into Otto's fur. I let myself feel the softness. There will never be another dog so handsome, unique, and distinct. And he's mine.

My head and my heart have declared a truce. They sing to me with their own music, and this is what they say: love is sometimes hard, but it is worth it, worth it, worth it.

CHAPTER 42

It takes all five of us to carry out the plan—six of us, really. It also takes a bit of luck.

Faith grasps a bag from Lulu's bakery.

Ray hoists several big containers from JoJo & The Earl's.

Tyler and Grant support an oversize box, struggling to keep it out of sight.

And I'm holding my gift for Gloria.

The receptionist at the check-in desk wears her hair in a twist. We tell her why we're there, and she frowns. "Is Ms. Crumb expecting you?"

"She prefers Gloria, actually. Gloria or nothing at all," I tell her as I sign in.

She narrows her eyes. "Do you each understand our visitors' rules? No noise, no firearms, no pets?"

We all nod, no one meeting her eyes.

"Yes, ma'am," Tyler adds for good measure.

Faith holds out the bag, smiling widely. "Muffins. I hope you and the other staff enjoy."

"How lovely," says the receptionist, peeking inside the bag. "No one ever brings things by for us."

We make our way across the lobby. Just a few more feet to the elevator, which is standing wide open. From inside the box, there's a scrabbling. We freeze.

"Achoo!" Ray says—the fakest fakey-fake sneeze I have ever heard in my entire life.

"Quiet, please," says the receptionist around a mouthful of muffin.

"Sorry about that, ma'am," says Tyler. "He's got allergies. Ragweed. Elephant grass. Pumpkin seeds."

Faith stifles a giggle.

"Mmm," says the receptionist.

We duck inside the elevator. Ray hits the button for the third floor.

From inside the box, there's a low whine. At the same time, all five of us say, "*Shhhh*."

"We'll be there soon," I say through the cardboard box.

The elevator dings, and we head down the hall. We look at one another with wide eyes. The plan is *working*.

We all know our parts. Tyler and Grant will station themselves as lookouts. If they see anyone coming, they'll hoot like owls. When I suggested this, Ray objected. Who ever heard of an owl in an old folks' home? But no one could think of anything better, so the plan stuck.

I can't wait to give Gloria her gift. I painted it last night. I take it out for a quick peek.

People see things in different ways. Some people might look at this picture and see a crabby lady, an ugly dog, and an unlucky girl. Others might see a woman who lives life on her own terms. A dog who is strikingly unique. A girl who is doing her best.

Some people might miss the small details—the crown on the old lady's head, the pom-poms on the wheel-chair, the eclipse of moths dancing around us. But there's no missing the deep-blue sky. I dotted it with stars like so many strings of twinkle lights wrapped around the universe.

Art is what you make of it. And I guess life is like that, too.

I can't say for sure whether these stars are lucky, but they're the only ones I've got. And I wouldn't change a thing.

ACKNOWLEDGMENTS

Mary Kate Castellani, who often knows what I'm trying to say before I do. Thank you for loving Annie from the start.

Marietta Zacker, who always goes above and beyond. I appreciate our talks and am very happy to have you in my corner.

A big thank you to Erin Casey, Nancy Gallt, and everyone at Gallt & Zacker. You are all stars!

Brigid Kemmerer, thank you for being there for me with every single page.

Thank you to Bloomsbury Children's Books: Cindy Loh, Claire Stetzer, Oona Patrick, Melissa Kavonic, Nicholas Church, Erica Barmash, Lily Yengle, Phoebe Dyer, Beth Eller, Jasmine Miranda, Faye Bi, Lex Higbee, Erica Loberg, Donna Mark, and Jeanette Levy. You are the best team I could ask for.

Gloria was inspired in part by my godmother, Barbara Sederquist, who was officially The Best. I'm thankful for all the wintergreen Life Savers, fireworks spectaculars, beach picnics, and of course her irreverent, tell-it-like-it-is personality.

Lisa Ramée, thank you for thoughts on early pages. Hoping for another lunch soon!

Lauren Tapyrik, thank you for sharing your heart. I loved hearing about your start with dogs.

Caroline Flory, your insight is priceless, as always.

Laura Case, thank you for being there through it all—the laughter, disappointment, joy, and the most dramatic seasons ever. Thank you to Jon, Nate, and Alex for your friendship.

Gauri Johnston, my sounding board, my reality check, my dear friend.

Aislinn Estes, for everything.

Anna Totten for many lunches, check-ins, and creativity pep talks.

Jared Turner, for being my brother.

Jackie Skahill, for helping me be a better writer and a better person.

Thank you Alicia Williams and Nailah Nolley, for our discussion about the importance of names in books. I appreciate you both so much.

Mariama Lockington, Jess Redman, Victoria Coe, Ashley Bernier, Jennifer Springer, Wendy Chen, Julia Ellis, Chris Kleinschmidt, Mandy Roylance, Larissa Marantz, Christina Haisty, Sam Boatwright, Lisa Ray, Camille Andros, Robin Hall, Kirsten Bock, Sarah Hall, and Stacy McAnulty, thank you for your friendship.

Chris Baron, Jessica Kramer, Rajani LaRocca, Cory Leonardo, Josh Levy, Naomi Milliner, and Nicole Panteleakos. Although we may disagree on raisins, we agree on so much more.

There are so many VERY GOOD DOGS and I would like to personally thank the following pups for making the world a better place: Friday, Abby, and Owen McDunn, Jack Gouthama, Pearl Johnston, Daisy and Charlotte Case, Lola, Bean, and Eva Estes, Beanie Gummadi, Justin Ellis, Daisy and Bowie Ellis, Pepper Chen, Dash Springer, Keva Totten, Cocoa Bernier, Boomer LaRocca, Winston and Indie Kleinschmidt, Buster McDonald, Scout, Piglette, and Bentley Hemingway, Louie Rustemeyer, and Sir Henry HoldLock.

Jon, Nora, Leo, and Violet—the stars that brought you to me were the luckiest ones to ever shine. I love you.